"My advice to you is leave."

Angela forced herself to meet His Excellency Sheikh Rashid al-Hazar's cold glance. "And why should I? You seem to be forgetting...your editor has offered me a job."

"A job to which you are not suited. Take my word for that, Miss Angela Baker."

"I'm sorry, I'm afraid I *can't* take your word. I happen to know that I'm perfectly qualified."

"Very well, then." He paused to fix her with a rapier look. "The suitability of your professional credentials is not in question. It is not for that reason that I am opposed to your appointment. The reason for my opposition is a great deal simpler—I do not like you, Miss Baker."

Stephanie Howard is a British author whose two ambitions since childhood were to see the world and to write. Her first venture into the world was a four-year stay in Italy, learning the language and supporting herself by writing short stories. Then her sensible side brought her back to London to study Social Administrations at the London School of Economics. She has held various editorial posts at magazines such as *Reader's Digest, Vanity Fair,* and *Women's Own,* as well as writing free-lance for *Cosmopolitan, Good Housekeeping* and *The Observer.* She recently spent six years happily trotting around the globe, although she has now returned to the U.K. to write romance novels.

Books by Stephanie Howard

HARLEQUIN ROMANCE

3093—MASTER OF GLEN CRANNACH
3112—AN IMPOSSIBLE PASSION
3153—WICKED DECEIVER
3195—ROMANTIC JOURNEY
3220—A MATTER OF HONOUR

HARLEQUIN PRESENTS

1273—BRIDE FOR A PRICE
1307—KISS OF THE FALCON
1450—A BRIDE FOR STRATHALLANE

DANGEROUS INFATUATION
Stephanie Howard

Harlequin Books

TORONTO • NEW YORK • LONDON
AMSTERDAM • PARIS • SYDNEY • HAMBURG
STOCKHOLM • ATHENS • TOKYO • MILAN
MADRID • WARSAW • BUDAPEST • AUCKLAND

Original hardcover edition published in 1991
by Mills & Boon Limited

ISBN 0-373-03237-4

Harlequin Romance first edition December 1992

DANGEROUS INFATUATION

CHAPTER ONE

STEPPING from the bookshop out on to the pavement was like stepping straight into the jaws of a bonfire.

Angela gasped and squinted up at the sky, a vivid slash of shimmering sapphire. Never had she seen a sky so blue nor felt a sun as fierce as the fiery red ball that beat down on this bustling little Arabian sheikhdom. And, for the thousandth time in the past ten days since her arrival in Jahira, she felt a thrill of wonder and excitement.

It was all so different, so unexpected. One felt that anything might happen in a place like this!

'Sorry, miss. I beg your pardon!'

In her moment of abstraction Angela had collided with a bespectacled young Indian in a grey safari suit, and clumsily dropped the newspaper she'd just bought.

She smiled apologetically. 'It was entirely my fault. I'm afraid I wasn't looking where I was going.'

The young man bent to retrieve her newspaper and handed it back to her with a smile. 'No problem,' he assured her, and with a nod he took his leave.

Angela pushed back her shiny blonde hair that fell to her shoulders in a wreath of soft curls and smiled to herself with quiet satisfaction. Like herself, the young Indian was a foreigner here, almost certainly, like Angela's engineer father, an employee of the wealthy Arab masters. And, like everyone else she had met so far, he had been friendly and helpful and polite. It just seemed to be a friendly sort of place.

Which was one of the reasons she had decided to stay on for a while and extend what had started out as a brief visit. For she had decided to take up the offer of a job.

That thought brought her urgently back to the present. For at half-past twelve she had a lunch date with the man who had made that tentative job offer—namely, the editor of the local English-language newspaper.

Angela glanced at her watch. It was almost quarter past twelve now, which meant she'd better get her skates on if she was to make it on time to the Al-Shaheen Hotel where they had arranged to meet!

But it was at that very moment, as she hurried across the pavement to where she had left her car at the side of the road, that she let out a moan of irritation. Somebody had boxed her in!

Damn it! How could they? How utterly thoughtless! How could anyone do such an infuriating thing?

But there were no two ways about it. They'd done it, all right!

Impotently, Angela stood for a moment to glare at the enormous gleaming white Cadillac that stood parked alongside her dusty hired Nissan, righteous indignation bubbling inside her. Whoever its owner was, he was both thoughtless and selfish, for it was obvious to anyone with a grain of consideration that there was no way she could get out with the Cadillac parked at her flank. There were cars parked behind her and cars parked in front of her. She was trapped like a sardine in a can!

And the culprit almost certainly had to be a man. Only the privileged male members of the local population drove luxurious cars like this in Jahira!

There were two Arab youths standing chatting on the pavement. 'I wonder if you can help me?' Angela appealed to them. 'Have you any idea who this car belongs to?'

The two boys shrugged. 'Sorry, we didn't see him.' Then in an effort to be helpful, one of them added, 'He's probably gone into one of the shops.'

That was a pretty fair assumption—but which one of the shops? Angela wondered. There were dozens lining both sides of the dusty, bustling street. And how long was Angela expected to hang around, melting in the ferocious heat of the sun, before the car's owner finally deigned to reappear?

Impatiently, she glanced around her, praying for him to materialise, for, apart from the discomfort of waiting in this heat, she simply couldn't afford a delay. The Al-Shaheen Hotel was ten minutes' drive away.

She approached the white Cadillac, her indignation growing, and circled it, searching for some solution to her dilemma. The driver's window had been left invitingly half-open and the key was still stuck temptingly in the ignition. And it occurred to her that nothing would be simpler than for her to slip into the driver's seat for a moment and move the wretched vehicle forward a couple of metres. Then she could extricate her own car, and neatly and quickly solve her problem!

But she hesitated to make so bold a gesture. For one thing, she was aware that she was far too conspicuous. A local might get away, unobserved, with such a ploy, but there was no such hope for a strikingly blonde English girl. And besides, she felt, it would be just a little cheeky.

She circled the car again, cursing softly, snatching angry glances at her watch. This lunch date was important and, anyway, it was bad manners to be late.

And then a thought occurred to her. She smiled to herself. Perhaps she could *summon* the owner of the Cadillac!

Judging by the way he had parked so hastily, the chances were that he was indeed in one of the nearby shops. Perhaps if she was to bang his horn a couple of times he would hear and come out to move his car for her. That was, she thought wryly, if he could distinguish his own horn from the cacophony of other horns blaring in the street. In Jahira everyone seemed to drive with one hand on their horn!

It was worth a try. With one final glance around her, Angela reached in through the open window and pressed the horn firmly. Ta-rah-rah! Then she pressed it twice again for good measure, straightened slowly, looked around her and waited.

Absolutely nothing happened. No apologetic rush of feet towards her, no guilty face peering at her from some doorway.

'Damn it, he must be deaf! I'll give him one more chance, and then I really will move the wretched car myself!'

Scowling crossly, she reached back inside the window, but even as her fingers hovered over the horn, Angela was aware of a sudden movement on the pavement. Instinctively she straightened, extracting her arms from the open window, and whirled round, feeling an unexpected stab of anxiety.

In the same instant a voice spoke to her, the tone harsh and cutting. 'What the devil do you think you're doing?'

He was somewhere in his middle thirties and dressed from head to toe in white in the traditional flowing *dishdasha* which fell to his ankles, and the elegant *kaffiyeh* or head-dress that was swept back across his shoulders. Only the cord that held the *kaffiyeh* in place was black—yet not half so black as the black look on his face.

He stepped down from the pavement and came towards her, like an alligator leaving a riverbank to enter the water, his movements sinuous and effortlessly graceful, yet with a sharp underlying sense of menace.

Just a couple of feet away from her, he came to a stop, a tall and faintly unnerving figure. 'Would you mind explaining to me what you were up to?'

What struck Angela most forcefully about him was the power in his face. A raw, undiluted, wholly masculine power that burned from every line of his strong-boned features.

It was there in the cruel curve of his nose, in the high smooth sweep of the intelligent forehead, in the shadowy dark cheekbones and the uncompromising chin. But most of all it shone like a beacon from the ferocious black daggers that were his eyes.

As those eyes drove into her, Angela took a step back and found herself wedged against the side of the Cadillac. Instantly she felt a flare of irritation with herself. Why was she acting so defensively when *he* was the one who'd committed a social misdemeanour? It was *he* who ought to be on the defensive!

She straightened and regarded him with defiant blue eyes, gesturing towards the long white limousine at her back. 'Is this your car?' she demanded without a flicker. 'Was it you who left it here?'

A pair of coal-black eyebrows lifted. Irritation sparked deep in the dagger-like eyes. 'Yes on both counts.' The eyebrows lowered. 'Have you something to say on the matter?'

It was a challenge, not a question, and Angela instantly rose to it. There was an arrogance in his manner that she found deeply annoying.

'As a matter of fact, I do,' she informed him coolly. He evidently thought that he could intimidate her, that she had no right to question him. But, though he looked as though he might devour her, she would not be bullied. 'Do you normally park your car in such a selfish fashion?'

Once more those expressive dark eyebrows lifted. 'Selfish, you say?' The words were tipped with steel.

'Selfish and totally lacking in consideration for others.' Angela nodded her blonde head towards the dusty Nissan. 'How was I supposed to get out?'

The black eyes briefly followed her gaze. 'Are you trying to tell me that that is your car?'

'That's precisely what I'm telling you. And, as you can see, you've boxed me in.'

He said nothing for a moment, just scrutinised her face. 'So, you would have me believe, then, that you are not a thief?'

'Thief? I'm no thief!' The accusation momentarily threw her. It had never crossed her mind that he might think such a thing! 'Why on earth should you suppose that I'm a thief?'

'You were half inside my car when I surprised you. What else am I supposed to think?'

'Well, I can assure you you're wrong!' Angela was suddenly grateful that she had resisted the temptation to climb into the Cadillac and move it forward a couple of feet. How would she have talked her way out of that?

She tilted her chin at him. 'It's a ridiculous accusation!'

He was standing over her, clearly unimpressed by her assurances. 'In Jahira theft is extremely uncommon, which is why we are able to leave our

doors and windows open without fear that our
valuables might be stolen. In your part of the world
things are rather different...' The black brows drew
together in menacing disapproval. 'Perhaps you
found the temptation of an open window over-
powering. There are many items of value lying
around in my car.'

He really meant it! Angela blanched a little. 'This
is utterly preposterous! I've told you I'm no thief!'

'Was it the gold key-ring you were after? Or
perhaps the crocodile-skin briefcase? Maybe it was
the car-phone that caught your eye?'

'Nothing caught my eye! How dare you accuse
me?'

'The street is so busy you thought no one would
notice, or that no one would dare apprehend a
beautiful young English girl.'

'I thought nothing of the kind!'

'But you timed it badly. Clearly, you did not
expect me to reappear so soon.'

'You've got it all wrong! That isn't what
happened!'

'Do you expect me to disbelieve the evidence of
my own eyes? Remember, I caught you with your
arm inside my car.'

Angela sighed and pushed back her hair. 'I know
what it must have looked like, but it wasn't like
that. I had my arm inside your car for a very different reason.'

The stranger's expression was openly sceptical.
'I would be most interested to know what that
reason might have been.'

So, at last, she was being given a chance to explain herself! Angela took a deep breath. 'It was all perfectly innocent. All I was about to do was bang on your horn in an effort to try and draw your attention. I'd already tried a couple of times— I wanted you to come and move your car—but apparently you didn't hear.'

'I see.' The black dagger eyes contemplated her for a moment, sweeping the length of her slender, long-legged form, flatteringly clad in a blue polka-dot dress. Then he narrowed his eyes thoughtfully as his gaze returned to her face. 'I see,' he repeated in a strange flat tone, as the dark eyes dissected, feature by feature, every honey-skinned centimetre of her delicately heart-shaped face.

Angela felt herself flush beneath the intimacy of his gaze, aware of the raw sexual power he seemed to radiate—a power that, in spite of herself, stirred something within her.

She pushed the feeling from her. 'As I was saying,' she reminded him, not quite managing to meet his eyes, 'there really was nothing sinister about my actions. All I was doing was trying to attract your attention.'

'Trying to attract my attention... Is that so?' There was an ambivalent edge to the way he said it that made Angela wish she'd chosen to express herself rather differently. Heaven forbid that he had got the impression that she was inviting him to make a pass at her!

But what came next took her totally by surprise, as in a tone as hard as crushed diamonds he accused her, 'So, you sought to summon me as one summons a servant? You expected me to leave whatever I was doing and come running at the double to do your bidding?'

Angela reeled a little at this unsignalled attack. 'Not at all,' she spluttered. 'That wasn't my intention.'

'I think it was.' He bridled visibly. 'I think that was *precisely* your intention.'

'I didn't mean to offend you.' Lord, but he was touchy! 'It was the only way I could think of getting you to come out and move your car.'

'Why didn't you just stand in the middle of the street and clap your hands?' he suggested sarcastically. 'That would appear to be the way you're used to behaving. You evidently expect everyone to be at your beck and call.'

'And you evidently expect everyone to wait on your convenience!' Suddenly Angela was through with apologies. He wasn't the only one who could fling accusations! 'How long was I expected to hang around until you finally decided to come back and move your car?'

'And how long exactly were you waiting? Half an hour? An hour, perhaps? Or was it even longer? It must have been quite a considerable time to have reduced you to such a state òf impatience.'

Of course, he was mocking her. He knew as well as she did that she had only been waiting a matter of a few minutes.

It was Angela's turn to bridle. 'That's not the point! I had no idea when you might choose to appear—and I happen to have a very important appointment.' As she said it, she glanced down quickly at her watch and felt her insides curl with annoyance. 'As it is, you've already made me late!' To her dismay it was just a couple of minutes to half-past twelve now.

'So, I am to blame for your tardiness, am I? I'm afraid I fail to see what it has to do with me.'

'Of course it's your fault! You're the one who's kept me hanging around here, wasting time with a load of useless explanations.'

'Not useless, I think. It was necessary for me to know what you were doing to my car.'

'Well, now you know. And if you hadn't parked it here so inconveniently in the first place I wouldn't have needed to go anywhere near it, and there wouldn't have been any need for explanations!'

'And if you had just exercised a moment's patience, instead of rushing to take measures which were really quite unnecessary, all of this could have been avoided.' He smiled, savouring the look of anger on her face. 'Just think,' he added to annoy her, 'had you been just a little less impatient you would long since have arrived to keep your appointment.'

Damn and blast him! He was enjoying rubbing her nose in it! 'Well perhaps, now that everything has been explained to your satisfaction, you would do me the favour of moving your car?'

With an impatient gesture Angela made to move past him, snatching the keys of the Nissan from her shoulder-bag. She was already late, of course, but perhaps it was still possible for her to make it to the Al-Shaheen Hotel before her host had actually finished his lunch!

But the tall stranger in the *dishdasha* was blocking her path. Co-operating with her wishes was evidently the last thing he intended. 'This appointment of yours,' he put to her now, his manner infuriatingly unhurried, 'must be very important for you to get so het up about it.'

'I'm not het up. I just happen to believe that it's good manners to be on time for an appointment. *Any* appointment, important or not.' There was no reason at all for him to know that this lunch date really did mean rather a lot to her. That would probably just make him even more uncooperative!

He shrugged his broad shoulders beneath the spotless white *dishdasha*. 'A very British attitude, if I may say so. In this part of the world punctuality is not considered so vital. Unless, of course, one has a meeting with the Emir.' He smiled amusedly, flashing strong white teeth. 'Is your appointment perhaps with the Emir of Jahira?'

'As a matter of fact, it's not.' Angela regarded him coldly, rewarding his blatant mockery with contempt. People like herself, as he was all too aware, did not have appointments with the country's ruler. 'But my appointment is none the less with a man of some standing.' Pointedly, she raised the newspaper in her hand. 'I'm having lunch with Mr Andrew MacLeish, the editor of the *Jahira News*.' Perhaps that would put this infuriating stranger in his place!

'The editor of the *Jahira News*?' He seemed to consider this information. 'So, you are a friend of the esteemed Mr MacLeish, are you?'

'No, not quite a friend.' In fact, she had never met him! 'My dealings with Mr MacLeish are purely professional.'

The black eyes narrowed. 'That is most interesting.' Then to her utter amazement, he stood aside with a flourish and invited her to pass in front of him. 'In that case, I shall hinder you no longer. As you say, Mr MacLeish is a man of some standing. It would be most inappropriate to keep him waiting.'

Angela didn't wait for a second invitation. Before he could change his mind she had swept swiftly past him and was jabbing the key in the door of the Nissan. If she had known that dropping MacLeish's name would have such an instantaneous effect she would have brought him into the conversation a great deal sooner!

The little hire car was like a furnace inside, the steering-wheel far too hot to touch. Hurriedly, Angela switched on the air-conditioner, letting the cool air circulate for a moment before pushing the scalding gear-stick into first.

And meanwhile, out of the corner of her eye, she watched as the tall stranger climbed into his Cadillac and pulled the big heavy door shut behind him. She could feel his eyes on her through the driver's window, but she would sooner have cut her head from her shoulders then turn round to meet that dagger-sharp gaze. All she wanted now was for him to drive away, and preferably with as little delay as possible.

Thankfully, he did not keep her waiting. A moment later the yacht-sized Cadillac was nosing its way into the stream of traffic, leaving Angela free to extricate herself at last.

She scowled as she headed towards the palm-lined Corniche and the glossy five-star Al-Shaheen Hotel that overlooked Jahira Bay. So much for her illusion that everyone here was friendly! She had just encountered the most uncivil individual that in all the twenty-six years of her life she had ever had the misfortune to cross swords with!

But at least there was one small consolation. She need never set eyes on the wretched man again!

'So, how would you feel about taking that on? I realise it would be quite a challenge.'

They were sitting over coffee in the sumptuous fifth-floor restaurant of the glittering Al-Shaheen Hotel—Angela and Andrew MacLeish, the editor of the *Jahira News*.

In spite of her arriving fifteen minutes late, the lunch with MacLeish had gone extraordinarily well. He had accepted her profuse apologies with a smile and assured her in his lilting Scottish accent, 'If you decide to stay on here you'll soon get used to dealing with situations like that. The locals are the loveliest people in the world, but they just don't share our Western concept of time.'

That was more or less what that infuriating stranger had told her, and it irked her to think that he had spoken the truth. In fact, every time she thought about him Angela felt irked!

Determinedly, she cast him from her thoughts. She would not allow him to ruin her lunch.

As it turned out it, it would have taken a very great deal to have ruined this particular lunch. The food was exquisite, a blend of Eastern and Western, and the setting, at a window table overlooking the bay, was as breathtaking as anything Angela had ever witnessed. The beauty of Jahira just kept on overwhelming her.

But perhaps even more breathtaking and overwhelming was the offer that Andrew MacLeish had just made her. She had expected to be offered a job as a reporter, but he had come up with something far more exciting. He had invited her to edit a new weekly women's page.

'How do you feel about it?' he was asking her now. 'Would you like to have a crack at it? Do you think you could handle it?'

'I'd love to do it! I'd love it more than anything!' Beaming, Angela leaned across the table towards him. 'And, yes,' she added, suppressing a small qualm of anxiety—as MacLeish had pointed out, the job would be a challenge, 'I think I could handle it. I'm certainly prepared to try.'

MacLeish smiled across at her. 'That's what I like to hear! Personally, I'm sure you'll make an excellent job of it. You have all the right experience, after all.'

Angela smiled back, flattered by his confidence in her, but felt moved to remind him all the same,

'I have plenty of experience of working for women's publications—but only as a freelance feature writer, not with the responsibilities of an editor.' Then she took a deep breath and confided frankly, 'But if you'll give me the chance I'll do my damnedest. The truth is I've been longing for an opportunity like this!'

'Then the job's yours, lass,' MacLeish assured her, 'and I couldn't be happier that you've said yes. I've been trying to get this women's page off the ground for more than eighteen months, but I just couldn't find the right person to do it. For this part of the world it's a bit of an innovation. It needs someone with plenty of journalistic experience—as well as plenty of sensitivity—to handle it.' He winked across at her. 'I know you're right for the job.'

Angela smiled, flattered. 'Thank you,' she told him. Then her expression sobered. 'I'm really very grateful. Apart from anything else, this job gives me the opportunity to spend a little more time here with my father. As you know, I came out to Jahira after he had that mild heart attack, and though he's back on his feet again I'm still a little worried about him—and he is all the family I have left these days...'

She broke off as a twist of pain touched her voice, then pulled herself together—she must not think of that now—and hurried on to assure MacLeish, 'All the same, I wouldn't consider taking on the job unless I was genuinely keen to do it. Though there is one thing I ought to point out...'

She took a deep breath. 'I have to be honest. I don't really see my future as being here in Jahira. Eventually, after a year at the very outside, it would be my intention to return to England.'

MacLeish nodded in agreement. 'That's fair enough. I can appreciate that not everyone wants to make their life out here.'

But there was more she had to make clear. Angela regarded him squarely. 'At the moment I'm totally won over by Jahira. But if, after a while, I were to discover that life here didn't really suit me, I would want to be free to return much sooner.' She cast a faintly anxious glance at MacLeish. 'Of course, I would quite understand if that's not acceptable.'

'Of course it's acceptable, and I appreciate your frankness. All I want is to get the page established.'

Angela looked him in the eye. 'How would it be if I agreed to stay for three months? That ought to be long enough to get the page going. Then at the end of the three months we can both review the situation.'

'You've got a deal!' MacLeish grinned across at her. 'And, now that that's settled, how soon can you start?'

Angela laughed, feeling a flutter of relief. 'I can start as soon as you like,' she told him.

'That's what I like to hear. How about next week?'

'Next week is perfect.'

'In that case, it's settled.' MacLeish reached out to shake her hand. 'I'll arrange for you to meet Sheikh Rashid before then.'

'Sheikh who?'

'Sheikh Rashid al-Hazar,' MacLeish explained. 'He's the owner of the *Jahira News* and he likes to meet all new staff members before they start. Don't worry,' he assured her, 'he's a very nice chap, considered to be the most eligible bachelor in Jahira. And your interview with him will be just a formality. He leaves all the hiring and firing to me.'

So the whole thing was settled. Angela could scarcely believe it. And she could hardly wait to get started in her new job.

'I'll give you a ring to let you know when Sheikh Rashid can see you,' her new boss promised her as they parted. 'It'll probably be within the next couple of days.'

And sure enough, just two days later, as she and her father were finishing dinner at home the phone in the hall began to ring.

'That was MacLeish,' her father reported a moment later when he came back from answering it. 'Apparently Sheikh Rashid wants to see you now. He's waiting for you at the *News*.'

Angela gaped at him in bemused disbelief. 'At this hour? The man's mad! Doesn't he know it's after nine o'clock in the evening?'

Her father smiled and shrugged. 'Nine o'clock or not, apparently he wants to see you right away.'

'Then he shall see me right away! Who am I to argue?' With a good-natured grin Angela jumped from her seat. 'All I need is five minutes to get changed!' Then, as she rushed off, she grimaced at her father over her shoulder, 'But I still think this Sheikh Rashid must be crazy!'

Ten minutes later, at the wheel of her hired Nissan, she was heading inland from Jahira City to the *Jahira News* offices on the edge of the desert. She had changed into a pretty cornflower-blue two-piece—with a slim straight skirt and an unfussy top—that she hoped was suitable for the impending interview.

MacLeish had said that this meeting with Sheikh Rashid was really nothing more than a formality, but the man was, after all, the owner of the newspaper and she was keen to make the right impression. And, besides, she found herself thinking just a little nervously, this would be her very first meeting with a sheikh!

It seemed no time at all before she was drawing up beneath the yellow neon sign announcing the *Jahira News*. Then she was hurrying down an air-conditioned corridor, following the signs to the editor's office. MacLeish had told her father that she should report to him first, then he would personally escort her to her meeting with Sheikh Rashid.

The butterflies that were building up in Angela's stomach dispersed momentarily at the sight of MacLeish's friendly face. He held out his hand to her. 'Good to see you again.' Then he was leading her back out into the corridor. 'Come on, my girl. Sheikh Rashid's waiting for you.'

It was only a short walk to the end of the corridor and a large door inscribed with the words

'Managing Director.' MacLeish tapped quickly and pushed the door open, stepping aside to allow Angela to pass in front of him.

'Sheikh Rashid,' she heard him say as she walked into the room, 'here's Miss Angela Baker to see you—the young lady who's going to transform our newspaper. If you don't mind, I'll leave you alone to get acquainted.'

A moment later the door closed behind him and Angela was standing alone in the middle of the room, feeling as though her legs had turned to stone beneath her.

She was aware that her jaw had dropped open foolishly and that every drop of blood had drained from her face. But there was nothing she could do but stand there like a zombie, transfixed by the piercing, dagger-like gaze of the man who sat waiting for her behind the desk.

CHAPTER TWO

SHEIKH RASHID AL-HAZAR rose slowly to his feet. 'So,' he observed drily. 'We meet again.'

Angela blinked at him, speechless for a moment. It was him, the man with the big white Cadillac, the man with whom she had crossed swords a couple of days ago and whom she had confidently expected never to see again.

His eyes were on her as, with a sabre-toothed smile, he extended one long-fingered hand in greeting. 'Funny, I had a feeling it would turn out to be you.'

Rarely had Angela felt at so severe a disadvantage as she moved stiffly towards him and accepted his handshake. This man, whom she had berated so frankly about his parking, accusing him of being selfish and lacking consideration for others, was not only a sheikh, a prince of the realm, but the owner of the company she was hoping to work for!

Talk about getting off to a bad start! She could scarcely have engineered a worse introduction if she'd tried!

As cool, strong fingers closed around her own, however—he had an eloquently masterful handshake, she observed—Angela snapped herself out of her momentary state of shock and decided to adopt a bold response, to treat him as she would any other mortal man.

She tossed him a wry smile and looked him straight in the eye. 'I wish I'd known who you were when we met the other day. I might not have been quite so hard on you,' she joked.

Sheikh Rashid al-Hazar did not smile in response. He regarded her for a moment through steely black eyes, then, inviting her with a brusque wave of his hand to sit in one of the deep leather armchairs opposite him, he resumed his own seat behind the huge desk.

He sat back in his seat and watched her for a moment, the deep jet eyes giving nothing away. 'And if you had known who I was?' he enquired in a cool tone. 'In what way would you have behaved differently?'

Angela felt her smile grow a little limp at the corners as she delved inside her brain for a suitable answer. For his enquiry, she sensed, was not some flippant, trivial question. On the contrary, he was putting her to some kind of test and she had no way of knowing what manner of response he was looking for.

'I'm not quite sure...' Playing for time, she sat back a little in her seat and adjusted the skirt of her dress over her knees.

There was no point in trying to give him the impression that she would meekly have allowed him to get off scot-free with the arrogant way in which he had treated her. He was quite obviously an intelligent and perceptive man who must have gathered for himself that she had more spirit than that.

'Let's just say,' she offered, accompanying her words with a polite smile, 'that I might have chosen to express myself a little less forcefully.'

'You mean you might have toned down your insults?' His tone was steely. 'That, Miss Baker, is quite a concession.'

'Well, you *were* in the wrong,' Angela responded too quickly. She bit her lip belatedly. 'What else was I supposed to do?'

'You could have thanked me for allowing you the privilege of being parked next to me. There are some I know who would have chosen that response.'

Was he joking or was he serious? It was impossible to know. The jet-black eyes gave nothing away.

'Well, I'm afraid I'm not one of them.' The very notion was distasteful. 'Sycophancy is not one of my strong points.'

'So I gather.' He smiled fleetingly. 'But do you not believe in showing respect for one's boss?'

'Of course I do!' This interview was becoming a minefield! 'But at the time I didn't know you were my boss. Believe me, I had no wish to offend you. I'm sincerely sorry if I did.'

She had no way of knowing whether her apology had been accepted. With an inscrutable smile and the faint lifting of one eyebrow Sheikh Rashid sat back a little in his seat and laced his long fingers across his chest.

He eyed her for a moment, then changed the subject. 'So, Miss Angela Baker...tell me something about yourself.'

A couple of days ago when she had first caught sight of him stepping towards her from the crowded public pavement, Angela's instant impression had been of vibrant, uncompromising power. Watching him now as he sat behind his desk, she found the impression was unchanged, merely subtly heightened. The sense of authority he exuded was so potent one could have reached out and touched it with a finger.

And it had nothing whatsoever to do with his being a sheikh. It was not the power of rank or any power that had been bestowed on him. It was a power that was a part of him, that seemed to flow from within him. If this man had been a beggar, one would still have sensed it.

As he waited for her to speak, Angela straightened in her seat. MacLeish had told her that he did all the hiring and firing, but nevertheless she had a growing suspicion that Sheikh Rashid was conducting a serious interview, that he needed to be satisfied that she was up to the job.

She regarded him squarely. 'What would you like to know?'

'Anything you care to tell me.' He smiled a brief smile that momentarily softened the harsh lines of his features. 'Perhaps,' he suggested, 'you could begin by telling me how you come to be in Jahira?'

Angela felt herself relax a little. At last, an easy question! 'I came out to spend some time with my father. He's a civil engineer. He's been out here for fifteen years. He's been in charge of the construction of a number of official buildings.'

'The hospital, the main post office and the university.' Sheikh Rashid had evidently been doing his homework. He nodded. 'Yes, I know. He's a very skilled man, and very highly thought of in Jahira.'

Angela smiled proudly at the compliment. It gave her a buzz to hear her father so lavishly praised. 'Thank you,' she answered. 'I'll tell him you said that.'

And as she shook back her hair, it crossed her mind that the high esteem in which Sheikh Rashid held her father undoubtedly wouldn't do her own case any harm. She relaxed a little more and confided, 'I'm looking forward to our working in the same part of the world for once, and I know my father's looking forward to it, too.'

But if Angela had dared to entertain the hope that she might be admitted on the coat-tails of her father, she was about to be swiftly and unceremoniously disabused. The man with the eyes that drove into her like daggers quite clearly believed in judging each case on its own merits.

Particularly her own case, she couldn't help suspecting.

He threw a sharp glance across the desk at her. 'And what special skills have you to offer Jahira that we should even contemplate offering you a position?'

'I'm a qualified journalist,' Angela answered swiftly. If before she had merely suspected that this interview was deadly serious, now she was absolutely certain of it! 'I've spent four years working for women's magazines in London.'

'As a freelance, MacLeish tells me.'

'That's right. As a freelance.'

'So, what's the matter?' He paused for a moment, his dark eyes as friendly as a desert rattlesnake's. 'Have you run out of commissions from these magazines you say you've worked for that you are suddenly so anxious to take a job in Jahira? Are your services no longer required in London?'

What a venomous remark! Angela winced inwardly, but was careful to answer him in unemotional tones. 'No, that is not the reason I want to work in Jahira. My journalistic skills, as it so happens, continue to be very much in demand in London.'

He regarded her for a moment, his dark eyes sceptical. 'Then what's the attraction of working in Jahira? It would surely be more appropriate for you to continue working in your own country?'

As Angela looked across into his face, framed by the delicate white *kaffiyeh* that was tossed back over his powerful shoulders, she could suddenly read the message in his eyes as plainly as if it were written there in English.

He did not want her to get the job. To dissuade her from taking it was the entire purpose of this interview.

'Why?' she asked him. 'Why do you say that?'
And why, she wondered inwardly, was he so dead
set against her?

'It is I who ask the questions. Your task is to
answer them!' In a sharp imperious gesture he un-
laced his fingers and laid them, palms down, on
the desk-top. Then, in case she had forgotten, he
sharply reminded her, 'I put it to you that it would
be more suitable for you to continue to work in
your own country. And now I am waiting for an
answer!'

Damned autocrat! Angela felt the flicker of an
urge to spring to her feet and walk out of the interview. Let him keep his damned job! she thought
on a wave of anger. Suddenly the thought of
working for this man seemed odious.

But she stayed where she was, instinctively
sensing that that was precisely the reaction he was
trying to provoke. With an effort she forced herself
to answer evenly, 'I hadn't forgotten your question,
Sheikh Rashid—and I can assure you I have every
intention of returning to work in my own country.'

She paused for a moment and deliberately held
his eyes, aware of a grim determination growing
within her to win this job in spite of him. Then she
smiled as she took contrary pleasure in clarifying,
'Eventually, but not just yet.'

'Am I to infer from that that you have other
offers of local work?' His response came back as
quick as whiplash.

Angela blinked. 'No,' she answered a little
lamely. 'No, as a matter of fact, I don't.'

'So, whether your return to England proves to be made "eventually" or somewhat sooner——' he held her eyes '—rather depends on your getting the *News* job?'

He might as well have said 'depends on me.' It was what he meant and it happened to be true. The chances of Angela's landing another suitable job in a country as tiny as Jahira, as they were both well aware, were virtually non-existent.

Angela met his eyes resentfully. Why was he being so hostile? 'Yes, I suppose it does,' she answered brittly.

He smiled at this admission, quite clearly enjoying the power they both knew he wielded over her. Then, still watching her, he dropped his hands from the desk top and laid them along the arms of his chair. 'So, tell me why you're so keen to remain in Jahira.'

Some instinct told her not to mention her father's health, but rather to keep her arguments strictly professional. Humanitarian considerations, she sensed, would not impress him.

She crossed her knees decorously. 'I find the job very attractive. That is what I want to stay on for.'

He was watching her closely. 'And what else?' he prompted.

Wasn't that enough? She scowled inwardly in irritation. Then she continued smoothly, 'Well, of course, it's also a chance for a rare experience. I've never worked overseas before.' She smiled as she added a little honest flattery. 'And I happen to find your country most fascinating.'

Sheikh Rashid, she was about to learn, was not an easy victim to flattery. He squashed her smile with a cool mocking glance. 'I see,' he observed cuttingly. 'You are looking for a little novelty.'

The man was merciless. In a few brief words he had succeeded in portraying her as both frivolous and shallow, scarcely qualities to be desired in a prospective employee.

'Not at all, Sheikh Rashid.' Angela kept hold of her anger. He would not trick her into talking herself out of this job! 'I merely recognise an opportunity to broaden my experience—a perfectly legitimate and desirable ambition for any serious journalist, as I'm sure you would agree.'

'A nice way of putting it.' He smiled his congratulations, but his eyes remained as cold as lumps of stone. Then, spreading his fingers along the chair arms, he put to her, 'Perhaps, since you bring up the subject of experience, this might be the moment for me to express an opinion. Namely that your professional experience, Miss Baker, seems to me to fall short of what is required for the job.'

Angela blinked at that. 'But that's not true! As I've told you, I've worked for four years as a professional journalist——'

'In London,' Sheikh Rashid finished for her. He smiled one of his hostile, sabre-toothed smiles. 'But Jahira, my dear Miss Baker, is a far cry from London.'

'I realise that.' Angela met his gaze steadily. 'But women are women the whole world over, and women's interest topics are my speciality. In my time

I've written on fashion and cookery, on bringing up children, and on women in the workplace—all the sorts of subjects that make up a women's page.'

She smiled to herself at the impassioned confidence of her argument. The natural nervousness she still felt at the responsibilities of editorship was something she would never reveal to this man!

Then she played her trump card. 'Besides, according to Mr MacLeish I'm ideally qualified to run this new women's page!'

But Sheikh Rashid had a trump card of his own, which he proceeded to lay now calmly before her. 'Mr MacLeish, as you will have realised, is a kind-hearted man. Of course he would wish to be polite to you.'

'Are you suggesting by that that he didn't mean what he told me? Are you suggesting that your editor was lying?'

'Absolutely not. Perhaps just stretching the truth a little.' Sheikh Rashid smiled a condescending smile. 'He and your father are very old friends. Perhaps he felt obliged to encourage you for your father's sake.'

What a preposterous suggestion! 'I hardly think so. The whole idea that I take the job was Mr MacLeish's in the first place. It wasn't I who went begging to him!'

'Perhaps your father begged for you.'

'I can assure you he didn't!'

'Perhaps he knew you were having difficulty finding work in London and felt it was his duty to help his daughter. I don't blame him in the slightest. He was merely trying to help you.'

'But he knew no such thing! It isn't true! I could have all the work I want in London! I don't need my father to go begging for jobs for me!'

'Then perhaps he had another reason for wanting you to get the job. How can you possibly know he didn't have a word in MacLeish's ear? After all, it's the sort of thing that fathers sometimes do, and they tend to do it without their offspring's knowing.'

Just for an instant he had almost succeeded in sowing a seed of doubt in Angela's mind. After all, her father was keen for her to stay on in Jahira, and, it was true, he and MacLeish were very good friends.

But just in time her instincts told her that this was merely a clever ploy to convince her she wasn't right for the job.

She took a moment to calm herself, then answered with dignity, 'Mr MacLeish offered me the job because he thought I could do it, not because he's a friend of my father.'

'You think so, do you?'

'I don't think so, I know so.'

'And do you think that he was right?'

'Yes, I do.' She looked back at him unflinchingly. 'I wouldn't have accepted his offer if I didn't.'

'Such confidence.' His tone was scathing.

'And why shouldn't I be confident?' Angela eyed him levelly. 'I've spent four years very successfully proving myself in one of the toughest journalistic centres of the world.'

He looked back at her in silence for a moment, then leaned towards her, gripping the arms of his chair. 'In that case, I would suggest,' he rapped at her impatiently, 'that, since you are such a success in London, you waste no more time in going straight back there!'

It was just at that moment that the office door opened and an exceedingly beautiful Indian girl, hair in a glossy black plait down her back, her slim figure dressed in a brilliant red sari, appeared in the doorway, carrying a tray.

'I've brought coffee, sir,' she explained to Sheikh Rashid with a deferential nod of her head as she came into the room and laid the tray on his desk.

'Very good.' His response was perfunctory and notably unaccompanied by even the flicker of a smile. He barely even bothered to say 'thank you' to the girl as she laid his coffee-cup before him then moved to the other side of the desk to place a second cup before Angela.

Angela deliberately caught her eye. 'That's very good of you,' she smiled. But though the girl acknowledged her politeness briefly, her attention had never really flickered from Sheikh Rashid.

'Will there be anything else?' she asked him now, hovering, waiting anxiously to do his bidding.

But with a wave of his hand Sheikh Rashid dismissed her. 'You may go,' he told her curtly.

The girl nodded. 'Thank you.' Then, palms together, fingers pointing towards her chin, she executed a series of graceful salaams as she retreated, backwards, out through the office door.

As she had watched the little ceremony, Angela was aware of the hairs on the back of her neck prickling in protest. The girl, presumably, was an employee, more than likely a secretary of some sort, and equally probably damned good at her job. Yet she had behaved, and been treated, like some lowly servant, a lesser being, undeserving of respect.

You silly girl, Angela chastised her inwardly. The days when women kowtowed to men—even to men who happen to be sheikhs!—thankfully, are gone forever. What you need, my girl, is a serious talking to, and I'm the very one to give it! Or I could let you read a couple of the articles I've written. They'd give you something to think about!

And it was in that very instant that she understood exactly what was behind Sheikh Rashid's hostility.

He had lifted his coffee-cup to his lips and was watching her carefully over the top of it. 'I hope Arabic coffee is to your taste. Some Westerners find it takes a bit of getting used to.'

'Really? I like it.' Angela glanced across at him, for the moment keeping her revelation to herself, and reached out to pick up her cup from the desk. The scent of the bitter brew, flavoured with aromatic cardamom seeds, rose deliciously to her nostrils. 'I very rarely drink anything else.'

Sheikh Rashid laid down his own cup with a click and smiled across at her, an alligator smile. 'Ah, yes, of course—your quest for novelty. And there is such a wide variety of novelties to be savoured here in the exotic and mysterious East. No doubt you find it all immensely entertaining.'

'I would say interesting more than entertaining.' So he was back on to that tack again! 'I enjoy finding out about new things. I suppose that's partly why I became a journalist.'

'In order to experience novelty?'

'In order to give free rein to my curiosity. Like most people who become journalists, I'm a naturally curious person.'

Sheikh Rashid smiled as his long brown-skinned fingers curled around the arms of his chair. 'How strange,' he observed, eyeing her beneath his lashes, 'that, in spite of this natural curiosity of yours, you have never taken the trouble to visit Jahira before. You had to wait until your father had a heart attack before, vulture-like, flying out here to be with him.'

Angela reeled at the crudity of his accusation. So, he had known all along of her father's illness and believed that she had come here in order to ingratiate herself and presumably stake her claim in his will.

It was a perfectly foul notion. She opened her mouth to tell him so. But before she could speak, he had cut in to accuse her, 'I am not mistaken? This is your first visit?'

'You are not mistaken, but——'

'That was what I thought. So, why is it that you have never come here before?'

Had she wished she could have explained that very easily, but it happened to be a very personal story which, quite frankly, was none of Sheikh Rashid's business.

With controlled anger Angela told him, 'I have my reasons, just as I have my reasons for having come now—reasons which, incidentally, are not those you suggested.' She squared her shoulders and turned caustic blue eyes on him. 'But why all these questions? It's no concern of yours why I've never made the trip to Jahira before.' As his eyebrows lifted just a fraction in surprise at this turnaround in the confrontation, she proceeded to surprise him even further.

'Are these diversionary tactics supposed to bamboozle me? Are they intended to put me off the track?' With a scornful little laugh she went on to inform him, 'If they are, I can assure you they have not succeeded. I know what this whole thing is really about.'

Sheikh Rashid straightened a little in his chair, his dark gaze shuttered as he invited her, 'What whole thing? Kindly enlighten me.'

'This silly interview, that's what whole thing.' Angela leaned towards him, suddenly enjoying her unexpected new sense of control. He had been giving her the runaround for quite long enough and it was high time the truth was out in the open. Damn the consequences! she decided, as she looked him straight in the eye and accused him, 'You don't want a women's page in your newspaper, do you? Why should you have a page for second-class citizens? That's the real reason for this ridiculous pantomime, so why not just be honest and come straight out and admit it?'

In the wake of her little eruption there was total silence. But it was a silence that clamoured and echoed eerily, like the silence that followed a shot from a gun.

As still as a falcon before it swoops on its prey, the man in the *dishdasha* on the other side of the desk regarded the blonde English girl with unblinking black eyes.

No doubt, thought Angela, trembling a little inwardly, she was the very first person in his entire life who had had the gall to accuse Sheikh Rashid al-Hazar, prince of the sheikhdom of Jahira, of being less than unquestionably and totally honest.

Her gall suddenly appalled her. Had she gone crazy? The very least her rash outburst was bound to cost her was this job that she was so anxious to have.

If he had risen to his feet and summarily demolished her, it would not have surprised her in the slightest. But he did no such thing. Instead he simply asked her, 'What makes you think that I don't want a women's page?'

Angela cleared her throat that had suddenly gone dry and answered in a tone of carefully balanced reasonableness, 'The way you keep trying to persuade me that I'm not really suitable for the job. We both know I am. I have all the right experience. You'd be hard pressed to find anyone with better credentials.'

'You think so?'

'I know it! And I think you know it, too. The real reason you're against me is because you don't want the page.'

Sheikh Rashid leaned back a little in his chair. 'If that were so, why would I have sanctioned the idea when MacLeish first came to me with his proposal for such a page?' He paused and assured her in tones of iron, 'Believe me, if I had been against the idea it would never have progressed beyond the drawing-board.'

'And it hasn't, has it?' Angela was quick to point out to him. 'According to MacLeish, it was eighteen months ago that he first put forward the idea. Eighteen months, if I may say so, is rather a long gestation period. My guess is that every time it's looked like happening you've deliberately done something to squash it. Exactly as you're trying to do now!'

'Then your guess is wrong, Miss Baker, I assure you. The page has never come close to happening for one simple reason: we have been unable to find a suitable editor.'

'How very convenient.' A new thought occurred to her. 'I'll bet that's why you agreed in the first place. Since there was nobody out here with the right experience, you felt it safe to assume you would never find an editor.' Her blue eyes threw him a look of pure challenge. 'You didn't reckon on someone like me coming along!'

'In that you are correct. I had not reckoned on such an annoyance.' His tone of voice was like a rumble of thunder. 'Your arrival in Jahira has been

most unfortunate. You would have done us all a
favour if you had stayed in England.'

Then, suddenly losing patience, he jerked to his
feet, sending the heavy leather armchair hurtling
back against the wall. 'However, you can still do
us all a favour—by booking a seat on the first plane
home!'

The ferocity of the gesture and the anger in his
voice caused Angela's heart to skip an anxious beat.
Then she stiffened inwardly as he swept round the
desk and came to stand directly before her. 'That
is my advice to you. Just kindly leave.'

Angela forced herself to look back at him
steadily. 'And why should I? You seem to be forgetting... your editor has offered me a job.'

'A job to which you are not suited. Take my word
for that, Miss Baker.'

'I'm sorry, I'm afraid I can't take your word. I
happen to know I'm perfectly well qualified.'

'You know nothing, Miss Baker.' His voice was
rough granite. 'Professional qualifications and
personal suitability are two very different and sep-
arate things.' As he spoke he swung away from her
to pace the carpet, his white robe billowing about
his tall frame, creating a draught that made the hairs
stand up on Angela's skin.

He paused suddenly to confront her. 'Would you
like me to explain?'

Angela sat very still. 'Yes, I would,' she
answered.

'Very well, then.' He resumed his pacing, cutting
the words at her across his shoulder. 'I am in perfect

agreement that you are qualified for the job. Even if I were permitted to recruit from overseas—which for such a relatively minor position would be against government policy—I would, as you say, be hard pressed to find better. The suitability of your professional credentials is not in question. It is not the reason that I am opposed to your appointment.'

He paused to fix her with a rapier look. 'The reason for my opposition is a great deal simpler—and I misled you merely to spare your feelings. I do not want you as editor of my women's page, Miss Baker, quite simply because I do not like you. I do not like your style. I do not like your attitude. I do not like one single thing about you!'

Talk about being blunt! Angela blinked at him disbelievingly. She had not been prepared for so barbarous an attack.

But, though her face had paled, she crisply pointed out to him, 'That strikes me as a rather unprofessional attitude. Surely your personal feelings about an individual shouldn't interfere with your professional assessment? You've already said I have the qualifications for the job. Surely that should be the only thing that matters?'

'Not so, Miss Baker.' His eyes had turned to daggers. 'You may have the *professional* qualifications for the job, but you have absolutely none of the *personal* qualities required. You are brash and insensitive and rude and impertinent! How MacLeish picked you for the job I shall never understand!'

'Perhaps because he's a better judge of character than you are!' Angela could feel a pulse of anger beating in her throat. Shakily she rose to her feet to confront him. 'I'm none of those things that you've just accused me of being—but I know perfectly well what's really worrying you! It's the fact that you think I don't know my place! You like women who are submissive, who bow and scrape. You're afraid of the sorts of things I might write in the women's page!'

'You're right, I am.' He ground the words at her savagely. Then he paused and looked down at her, his lips curling cruelly, the black eyes narrowing as he reminded her, 'But we are being a trifle premature. You have not yet been appointed to the position in question.'

'I have as good as!' Angela was defiant as she tilted her head to glare up into his face. 'Mr MacLeish has offered me the job and I've accepted it. I'm afraid there's not a single thing you can do about it—unless you care to override your editor's authority!'

When he did not answer, Angela could sense that he would be reluctant to take so drastic a measure. From the way MacLeish had spoken of their relationship, the owner and managing director of the *Jahira News* and its highly esteemed and long-standing editor did not interfere in one another's realms of influence. And besides, MacLeish was not a man to be pushed around.

'Like it or not, it seems you're stuck with me,' she took pleasure in pointing out to him with a triumphant little smile.

To her surprise, Sheikh Rashid returned her smile, though its corners were dipped in purest vitriol. 'We shall see,' he purred softly. Then he took her by the arm and started to lead her towards the door. 'There is some way to go yet before this story is ended. It would be unwise, at this point, to predict its outcome.'

'And what is that supposed to mean?' Was she being subtly threatened?

He glanced down at her as he reached with his free hand for the door-handle, the fingers around her arm momentarily tightening.

'If you really want to find out, go ahead and take the job. But if you prefer an easier, shall we say, less troublesome life, take my advice and go back home to England.'

Then he pulled the door open and released her abruptly. 'Think about it. Most carefully,' he advised her.

A moment later, as the door closed behind her, Angela found herself standing, stunned and speechless, out in the empty office corridor.

CHAPTER THREE

THE official behind the desk shrugged and shook his head. 'Sorry,' he said, 'but we require written testimonials before we can supply you with a Residence Permit.'

'But I've been coming here for days and you've never said that before! Why are you making everything so difficult?'

The official shrugged again in the face of Angela's protests and raised one hand to adjust his *kaffiyeh*. 'It is not I who make the rules,' he offered reasonably. 'My job is simply to follow the instructions of my superiors.' Then he smiled suddenly and leaned towards her. 'Would you like more coffee, Miss Baker?'

With a gasp of impatience Angela rose to her feet. The hospitality of the Jahirans, she had learned, was boundless—everywhere you went you were instantly offered coffee—but it wasn't hospitality she was looking for; what she needed was her permit!

Still, she managed a polite smile. 'No, thank you,' she answered. As he had pointed out to her, her problems weren't his fault—although she had a shrewd suspicion she knew whose fault they were!

She sighed as she started to head for the door. 'I'll see what I can do about getting these testimonials.' Then she bade him goodbye. *'A'salam u'alaikum.'*

Outside the Immigration Department building the sun was beating down with its usual ferocity, sending the pedestrians scurrying for the few patches of shade. Angela smiled to herself, momentarily forgetting her irritation. It was hard to believe that this was early February!

But instantly her anger came rushing back on her. By now she should have been officially established in her new job—for, to all intents and purposes, the job was hers.

She had emerged from that confrontation in Sheikh Rashid's office slightly stunned but determined to ignore his harsh warning. He'd been trying to scare her off for his own base reasons and she would be damned if she would give him the pleasure of seeing her back down.

She'd repeated nothing to MacLeish of what Sheikh Rashid had said to her, partly because her pride would not allow her—his insults had been mean and hurtful and cruel—and partly because she feared that with too much candour she might simply make the situation worse.

'He seemed less than enthusiastic,' was how she'd put it when MacLeish had asked her how the interview had gone.

To her relief, MacLeish had shrugged. 'He's just being cautious. As I told you, this is a sensitive area. But I have every faith in you.' He threw her a wink. 'So, that's settled, then. You can start next week. Have a word with my secretary and she'll explain to you how to go about getting the documents you'll need.'

As Angela frowned, he went on to explain, 'First and foremost, you'll need a Residence Permit—you can't join the staff until you've got that. Then you'll need to sort out a local driving licence. So far you've been driving on your UK licence, but you can only do that for up to fourteen days. And a driving licence is essential in Jahira. As you know, there's no public transport, and taxis, when you can find one, are horrendously expensive.

'But don't worry, lass——' he'd smiled reassuringly '—most people have their documents within a couple of days.'

Most people, perhaps, but predictably not Angela! She scowled to herself now as she stepped to the edge of the pavement and scoured the street impatiently for a taxi. Ten days had passed since that conversation with MacLeish and she was still without either of those vital documents. And, though she had refrained from voicing her suspicions to anyone—for, instinctively, she knew that no one would believe her—she was certain she knew who she had to thank for that.

His Excellency Sheikh Rashid al-Hazar!

It was obvious what he was up to. He was hoping he could persuade her that the job simply wasn't worth all the bureaucratic hassle, that she ought to throw in the towel and head back to London.

And, to be truthful, that solution was starting to have its attractions. Her thankless daily visits to chase up her documents were proving about as effective as a toothpick against a mountain. Quite frankly, she was making no progress at all.

To her astonishment a taxi suddenly appeared and instantly she reached out to wave it down. A moment later she was clambering inside and the driver was turning round to her as he switched on the meter. 'Where to, miss?' he enquired.

As the clock started to tick, Angela felt her anger strengthen. This daily pantomime had cost her a fortune in taxis and suddenly she had had enough!

She hesitated for just a fraction of a second, abruptly rejecting her plan to go straight home. Then with a grim smile she sat back in her seat and instructed, 'Take me to the Al-Hazar Tower!'

She had some gall—Angela realised that—even to think of confronting Sheikh Rashid al-Hazar in the fifteen-storey office block that bore his name. For within its sumptuous walls he was not merely the managing director of the modest but respected *Jahira News*; he was the president of the mighty al-Hazar Corporation, one of the biggest oil companies in the Middle East.

For Sheikh Rashid's main business, Angela had discovered, was oil. The *News* was little more than a hobby to this man who daily transacted business deals worth millions of dollars.

And by day it was the oil business that occupied his time. Only in the evenings did he concern himself with his newspaper. So now, at four in the afternoon, it was at the Al-Hazar Tower that Angela would find him.

In no time at all they were drawing into the tower forecourt. Angela thrust a pile of banknotes at the cab driver. 'Keep the change!' she urged him and jumped out.

Then she was striding through a vast marble-floored reception hall and taking the lift to the fif-teenth floor.

'Is His Excellency expecting you?' a secretary asked her, frowning over the entries in a huge ap-pointments book.

'Not exactly, but I'm sure he'll agree to see me,' Angela assured the girl with more confidence than she felt. All at once, in these grand and unfamiliar surroundings, she was starting to wonder if she wasn't being a little rash.

'Just a moment. Take a seat.' The receptionist waved at a large leather sofa, then disappeared swiftly through a glass-panelled door.

Angela sat down stiffly, her nervousness growing. He'll probably refuse to see me, she consoled herself cravenly. And maybe, after all, that might be a good thing. Here, on his own ground, where he ruled absolutely, might not be the best place in the world to confront him.

But then she heard a swish as a door behind her opened, and she spun round automatically, rising to her feet, as a deep voice commanded, 'You'd better come in!'

He was standing in the open doorway to his office, looking about as welcoming as a one-man firing squad, the sides of his head-dress thrown back from his face, his strong arms folded across his chest. 'Well? What are you waiting for? I told you to come in.'

It was something about the all too familiar arrogance of his manner, as he stood aside to let her pass, that snapped some switch inside Angela's head. All her nervousness instantly fled from her. Fearlessly, she looked back at him. 'How very hospitable of you.' Then, head held high, she swept into the room.

His office was huge, with a huge mahogany desk, and a huge plate-glass window overlooking the bay. Angela strode halfway across the acre of red carpet, then paused to observe, as he came to stand behind her, 'You certainly seem to believe that big is beautiful. Is everything about you on such a grand scale?'

As she turned to glance at him, the dark eyes fixed her. 'It might be,' he answered, his tone enigmatic, causing a faint but foolish blush to touch her cheeks. Then, detaching his eyes, he swept arrogantly past her. 'Perhaps, once you have finished paying me compliments, you would like to explain what the devil you're doing here.'

He was standing behind his desk now, totally dominating its vastness. Then, pointedly, he seated himself without inviting her to do likewise.

'Don't worry, I didn't come here to pay you compliments.' Angela straightened her shoulders beneath her navy linen dress. 'I came here for a very different purpose.'

'Namely?'

'Namely this.' She pushed back her hair. 'To ask you to stop opposing my appointment to the *News*.'

Rashid smiled sarcastically. 'I thought the job was yours. I thought you told me that MacLeish had offered you the job and that there was nothing I could do about it.'

Angela's answering smile was equally sarcastic. 'And you warned me that if I took the job it was within your power to make my life "troublesome".' She paused a beat before confessing in a wry tone, 'It seems that I was wrong and you were right.'

Sheikh Rashid flicked back the sides of his *kaffiyeh*. 'I think you will discover that that is generally the case. You have done well to learn your lesson so quickly.' He held her eyes for a meaningful moment. 'Now you would be wise not to forget it.'

Inwardly Angela gritted her teeth. He was the most arrogant man she had ever encountered, but she must suppress the irritation he provoked in her if she was to make any headway in winning him round.

Calmly she seated herself in one of the jade damask armchairs that were arranged around the front of the huge desk. 'Shall I tell you how I've spent my day?' she put to him.

He looked surprised. 'And why should that interest me?'

'Because it's thanks to you that I spent it as I did.' She crossed her knees, keeping her eyes fixed on him, and elaborated in a cool and steady tone,

'This morning I spent three hours at the Traffic Police Department, trying, unsuccessfully, to sort out my driving licence, while this afternoon I spent another two hours, which were equally wasted, at the Immigration Department. It seems that no one wants to co-operate in supplying me with the documents I need to take up my position at the *News*.'

'How very unfortunate.' He smiled a cobra smile. 'In that case, I would strongly advise you not to continue wasting your time in this manner.'

'You mean go back to England?'

'That would be a sensible solution.'

'But I've already told you I don't intend doing that.' Her voice rose on a note of determination as she said it, causing his eyebrows to lift a little. 'And that's why I've come here now to see you. You're behind this conspiracy, aren't you?' she accused. She had no proof, but she knew it was so.

Predictably, he smiled at her allegation. 'What conspiracy?' he enquired smoothly. 'I fear you're letting your imagination run away with you.' Then he threw her a cutting look. 'You surprise me, Miss Baker. I would have thought that a supposedly competent young woman like yourself would have had no difficulty in sorting out her documents. The procedure, after all, is perfectly straightforward.'

'I'm surprised you're surprised!' Angela blanched at the gall of him. 'Considering it's all thanks to you that I'm having problems!'

He ignored her accusation and put to her instead, 'Have the authorities, then, refused your applications?'

'Not openly, no. But they're imposing endless conditions. The Traffic Police are saying I'll have to sit a driving test and apparently there's a waiting list of weeks! And, as far as my Residence Permit is concerned, the Immigration people are insisting that I produce a whole sheaf of certificates and testimonials to prove that I'm qualified for the job on the *News*.'

'So, what's the problem? Don't you possess such testimonials?'

'Of course I do, but I don't have them here with me!' Angela glared at him. 'As you guessed, they're in London. I wasn't planning on applying for a job when I came here, so naturally I didn't bring them with me.'

'How very tiresome.' Rashid frowned in mock sympathy. 'However, I'm sure you can see the point of view of the authorities. They have a right, after all, to ascertain the calibre of any alien seeking employment in Jahira.'

'But everyone knows I'm qualified! Even *you* admitted it! Nothing of what they're demanding is the least bit necessary!'

'That is not for me to say.' Rashid shrugged infuriatingly. 'It is not for me to tell the Immigration Department its job.'

Angela clenched her fists. She was getting nowhere. 'How can you say that when it was you in the first place who instructed them to demand these conditions?'

'I?' He regarded her through dark, shuttered eyes. 'I assure you, I do not run the Immigration Department.'

'But you do have influence!'

'I would not deny that.'

'And you're not above using it.'

'In certain cases.'

'Like mine, for example. You're out to thwart me, aren't you? Without a Residence Permit I can't join the *News*'s staff!'

'I'm afraid the situation is more serious than that.' Rashid smiled a callous smile as he proceeded to point out to her a bitter truth of which she was already aware. 'Without a Residence Permit you cannot remain in Jahira beyond a maximum of six weeks. If you seriously wish to remain in our country, Miss Baker, I would advise you to get hold of these documents without delay.'

'If only I could!' As he rose to his feet and turned his back to her to stare out the window, apparently bored with the whole exchange, Angela was suddenly overcome by a sense of helplessness. The documents she needed were in a file in her flat in London, and the only person who could get hold of them for her was her next-door neighbour, who was on holiday in Austria.

And it just wasn't fair! Thanks to Sheikh Rashid, she was going to end up being forced to go back to England.

Both her father and MacLeish had already done their utmost to try and cut through the red tape for her. There was no one else who could help her now.

Except Sheikh Rashid. And herself, of course.

She rose to her feet and took a deep breath. As hopeless as it looked, she couldn't just give up. She had set her heart on the challenge of the women's page—and, perhaps even more tellingly, on the challenge of beating Sheikh Rashid.

Facing his broad shoulders, she forced herself to plead a little. 'Why won't you relent? Just give me a chance. You'll see you've been wrong in judging me so badly.'

'Somehow I doubt that.'

'You *will* see, I promise you.' She took a step towards him. 'Please give me a chance.'

He had evidently been unaware of her approach, for he turned now, abruptly, and collided with her roughly, almost knocking her to the floor. Instantly, with both hands he reached out to grab hold of her, the fingers of one hand gripping her by the arm, the other hand around her shoulder, steadying her against him.

'Are you OK?' He looked down into her face as, still gasping a little from the shock of the collision, Angela sank unresistingly against him.

And suddenly her heart was beating like a tom-tom. She blinked up at him foolishly. 'Yes, I'm OK.'

He was frowning down at her as he continued to hold her, but, subtly, his expression had changed. 'Why won't you just go back to England?' he insisted. 'Go back to your family, your boyfriend, your friends.' This time it was he who seemed to be pleading.

Angela swallowed. 'I have no family. I have no boyfriend.' She could feel his warmth through the cotton *dishdasha*. She could even, she fancied, feel the beat of his heart.

'Everyone has a family.' His gaze was intently on her, and, this close, his eyes were as black as midnight and fringed with lashes that could make the stones sigh. And his skin had a clean, musky masculine scent that filled her nostrils and made her head swim.

'The only family I have is my father. My mother died just over a year ago and my only sister lives in Australia.'

'Your mother died?' He seemed to sense the shaft of pain in her. Just for moment his arms held her more closely. 'That is sad for you, and sad for your father. I had no idea. I apologise,' he told her.

'My parents were divorced. They'd been divorced for many years.' Why was she telling him this? And why did she assure him, 'That's part of the reason I never came to Jahira—not because I wasn't interested in my father or how he lived. But I grew up with my mother. I saw my father only occasionally.'

'I see.' He looked at her in silence for a moment, and there was a warmth and a compassion in his eyes that overwhelmed her. Then, all at once, like a mantle falling from her shoulders, he loosed his grip and stepped away from her. 'Still, now that you've had a chance to spend some time with him, I really think that you should go back.'

A barrier had fallen. His expression had grown cold again, and he informed her now in uncompromising tones, 'You're not the kind of woman I want working for the *News*.'

The sudden change in him was shattering, like a bucket of icy water thrown in her face. Angela clenched her fists and instantly retaliated. 'Oh, I know the kind of women you like to have around you—obedient little slaves that you can boss about and bully, the sort of women who would never dare to answer you back! Well, you're right—I'm not like that, thank heavens!'

Sheikh Rashid al-Hazar regarded her in silence. Throughout her little outburst his expression had never altered. 'You're referring to my secretary, Lalitha,' he said at last. 'You disapprove of the respect with which she treats me?'

'That's not respect!' Angela had a sudden image of the beautiful subservient Indian girl she had met briefly in the *News* office. 'That's what I would call servility!'

'You think, perhaps, that she should behave more as you do?'

'A little more assertiveness wouldn't do her any harm.'

'It might even improve her, you think, no doubt. Has it not occurred to you, Miss Baker, that you may have something to learn from her?'

'As a matter of fact, it hasn't.' Angela's tone was brittle. 'I can assure you I have no intention whatsoever of salaaming backwards out of your office door!'

'I'm sure you haven't.'

'You can count on it!'

He paused for a moment. 'I think you've proved my point. You're totally out of place here, Miss Baker. Take my advice and go back to England.' Then, before she could answer, he was sweeping towards the door. 'I think our business is now concluded.'

As Angela glared back at him, hating him, loathing him, he reached for the door-handle and pierced her with a look. 'Since I have no intention of changing my mind, you need not waste any more of your time. Or mine,' he added, pulling the door open. 'My secretary will call you a cab if you wish.'

His arrogance was overwhelming. Angela felt rage burn within her. On stiff legs she crossed the carpet towards him. 'You're not going to get rid of me as easily as you think! I shall speak to the British Ambassador! I'll speak to the Minister of Immigration!' As she came to stand before him, she glared into his face. 'You're not the only one with influence in Jahira!'

He did not flinch. He simply held the door wider. 'Goodbye, Miss Baker. It's been a pleasure, as always.'

Just a couple of days later, there was the strangest development. A phone call from the Traffic Police Department to inform her that her driving licence was ready and waiting to be picked up.

Angela was there within the hour. Then, with the precious document tucked safely in her bag, she went straight to the car-hire company to hire back her red Nissan.

At last she was mobile! She felt like cheering. Now she could get on with some of those freelance articles that MacLeish had said she could work on till her Residence Permit came through.

The very next day, brimming with enthusiasm, she was at the desk she had been lent in a corner of the *News* office, working on her first article and getting to know the staff.

It was Lalitha, the beautiful young Indian secretary—who worked for MacLeish as well as Sheikh Rashid—who took it upon herself to show Angela round.

'It'll be lovely having you here,' Lalitha confided to her warmly. 'I've been the only female on the staff until now. I'll enjoy having someone I can chat to.'

Angela smiled back at her with genuine liking. 'I'm looking forward to it, too.' And privately she observed that from now on Lalitha would have more than just someone to chat to—she would have someone to help her stick up for herself against Sheikh Rashid!

Not that she had any intention of crossing Rashid's path any more than she absolutely had to. That sort of aggravation was something she definitely didn't need! And, since most of her dealings would be with the editor, there would be mercifully little call for her to go anywhere near the managing director.

What was more, she discovered, if she was careful she could virtually avoid ever being in the office at the same time as him. Lalitha had told her he usually arrived about eight and stayed on till around midnight when the paper was put to bed.

I'll make sure I'm always out of the office by half-past seven—at the latest! Angela decided.

But she ought to have known he wouldn't stick to his routine, especially when it suited her so well. Sooner or later he was bound to surprise her. And, as bad luck would have it, it proved to be sooner.

She was just leaving the office as usual one evening and making her way to the floodlit car park when a long white Cadillac came sweeping through the gates, heading for the row of private parking spaces.

'Blast and damnation!' Angela cursed to herself. 'Trust him to turn up early!'

Her own car was parked at the other end of the car park—a habit she had adopted to reduce the risk of bumping into him. Perhaps, she decided now, hunching a little, she could sneak her way between the other parked cars and reach the red Nissan before he had noticed her.

But she was less than halfway there when she heard him call out, 'So, you're still here, are you, Miss Baker? I thought you might have gone home by now.'

Angela swung round, feigning total unconcern at this highly irritating encounter. 'I'm just on my way home, as a matter of fact. This is the time I usually leave.'

He had come striding across the tarmac to stand before her, the white *kaffiyeh* blown back from his face. He smiled without humour. 'You misunderstand me. When I said "home", I was referring to London.'

The hostility in his words momentarily threw her. She had been made to feel so welcome by everyone on the paper that she had almost forgotten that its owner detested her.

But she looked back at him steadily. 'Why should I return to London when I happen to have a good job right here?'

'You mean these bits of freelance stuff you're doing? I wouldn't really call that a serious job.'

'I wasn't meaning the freelance,' Angela crisply corrected him. 'The women's page editorship is the job I've been offered, and I'll be taking it up as soon as my permit comes through.'

'You mean it hasn't come through yet?' He raised mocking black eyebrows. 'What happened? Weren't the British Ambassador and the Minister of Immigration able to assist you, after all?'

Angela grimaced pointedly at his sarcasm. He was referring to that threat she had made in his office. But she had known even then that the Ambassador couldn't help her and that she had as much hope of speaking to the Minister as to the man in the moon.

She threw him a cool look. 'I didn't waste my time with them. I know perfectly well that it's all down to you.' She smiled sarcastically. 'It was very decent of you, by the way, to allow me to have a driving licence. What on earth prompted that act of human decency?'

He smiled an amused smile, but did not answer her. 'I calculate you have about two weeks left before your visitor's visa runs out and you have to leave us. Unless, of course, you've managed to lay your hands on these testimonials.'

Angela's lips thinned resentfully. How he was enjoying tormenting her! 'Not yet,' she answered coldly. 'I'm still working on it.'

'What a pity.' He smiled and began to turn away, pausing briefly to advise her over his shoulder, 'Enjoy your stay at the *News*, Miss Baker. But don't bother carving your initials in your desk. I fear it may not be yours for very much longer.'

Then he was sweeping off, his head-dress billowing out behind him, leaving Angela glaring after him in impotent rage.

But what happened next was sadly destined to drive all thoughts of Sheikh Rashid from Angela's head.

First there was the phone call from the hospital. 'You'd better come at once. Your father's had another heart attack. He's in a serious condition in Intensive Care.'

Then there was the rush to his bedside and an anxious three-day vigil until his condition finally stabilised.

It was on the third day that she bumped into MacLeish in the hospital corridor, on his way to visit her father. As she was thanking him for the concern he'd shown during the crisis, he cut in kindly, 'No need to thank me. That's what friends are for.' Then he touched her arm. 'Oh, by the way... I didn't bring it up before because you had too much on your mind, but your Residence Permit came through the other day.'

Through the fog of anxiety that clouded her brain, Angela looked back at him. 'Are you serious?'

'Never more so. Congratulations. You're now officially a member of the *Jahira News* staff.'

'But what about Sheikh Rashid? Didn't he object?' She couldn't believe what she was hearing.

'Of course he didn't. Besides, he's gone to Europe for a couple of weeks.' MacLeish smiled kindly at her bewildered expression. 'You can get started on the women's page whenever you feel like it.'

Angela got started that very same day, throwing herself enthusiastically into all that the job entailed. When she wasn't at the hospital she was rushing around Jahira, gathering stories for her weekly page.

But in one corner of her mind she was making no assumptions regarding the permanency of her new job. Sheikh Rashid, she had calculated, had already left for Europe when her Residence Permit came through. Otherwise, she was certain, it would never have been issued. And she was not at all confident that, when he returned, she might not discover that it had been revoked.

Remembering his advice, she had cautiously refrained from carving her initials in her desk.

It had been a particularly busy week on the evening that Vince, the *News*'s senior photographer, dropped Angela off at the office after a joint assignment so that she could pick up her car.

'I've got another job,' he told her. 'A reception for some visiting American dignitaries. But, if I'm not too late, I might drop by to see you. I'll be in your area anyway.'

Angela smiled back at him. 'I'd be delighted to see you.' A bit of company for the evening would make a pleasant change.

Back at the villa she showered and changed—into a loose turquoise kaftan—and tied back her hair. But when by ten o'clock there was still no sign of him, Angela decided he probably wasn't coming.

She tossed aside the magazine she'd been reading. She might as well take herself off to bed.

But it was at that very moment that the doorbell rang. With a pleased grin Angela jumped to her feet. It was a little late, but better late than never!

She hurried into the hallway to open the front door. 'I'd just about given you up!' she laughed. But the smile froze on her lips as she looked into the face of the tall dark man who was standing there.

'Good evening, *habibiti*,' he greeted her.

It wasn't Vince.

Of all people, it was Rashid!

CHAPTER FOUR

THE way her heart had leapt at the sight of him was shocking. A ridiculous warm glow went spreading through her.

How preposterous! she chastised herself, pulling herself together. Anyone would think you were happy to see him!

'Well, are you going to keep me standing on the doorstep, or do you intend to ask me in?' The question was really quite superfluous, for before she could answer him he had swept into the hall.

Angela glared at him, her emotions returning to normal. 'What are you doing here?' she demanded hotly. It was a positive relief to feel annoyed with him again.

'I've come to tell you to pack a case.' The black eyes were unblinking. 'You're moving out of here immediately.'

Angela frowned up at him. 'Moving out of here? What the devil are you talking about?'

'Surely that was plain enough?' He spoke with impatience. 'Go and pack a case. You're coming with me.'

'I'm doing no such thing!' She straightened and scowled at him. 'Have you gone out of your mind, barging in here at this time of night, making such ludicrous demands?'

'Believe me, they're not ludicrous. They are perfectly sane and serious. You are to come with me and you are to come immediately.' He gave an imperious nod in the direction of the bedrooms. 'I suggest you go and pack some things.'

Did he seriously expect her to snap to and obey him? From the tyrannical look that was etched on his face, Angela deduced without difficulty that he did. She took pleasure in sweeping past him and heading, not for her bedroom, but for the kitchen at the other side of the house.

'Sorry, but I'm afraid packing is not on my agenda. I was just about to make myself a bedtime drink.'

'You can have a drink where you're going.' He had followed her to the kitchen. 'Kindly don't waste time. Just get ready to leave.'

He evidently had not heard her, or else he thought she was joking—but he was about to discover that she was deadly serious.

Turning her back on him very deliberately, Angela took a pan down from the shelf, laid it on the stove and crossed to the fridge. Yet, though she had not the faintest intention of going anywhere with him, one tiny corner of her mind was curious.

'The question is purely academic,' she assured him over her shoulder, 'but, just out of interest, where were you planning on taking me?'

'Not "were", *habibiti* . . .' Rashid smiled without humour, his use of the word *habibiti*, Arabic for 'my dear', clearly intended solely to irritate her. 'You may be making a good job of gaining a little time, but my plan to remove you from this villa remains unaltered. With your father in hospital, you cannot remain alone here. I'm afraid I absolutely forbid it.'

Forbid it, indeed! Who did he think he was talking to? His two weeks in Europe had done nothing to mellow him. He was as irritating and as arrogant as ever!

Pointedly ignoring him, Angela opened the fridge and lifted out a carton of milk.

He took a step towards her, causing her to tense, but his tone had softened markedly as he told her, 'I just got back and they told me about your father. All I can say is that I'm sincerely sorry and that I shall ensure that he receives the best possible medical attention.'

'He's already receiving that without your intervention.' Angela threw him a hard look from under her lashes as she laid the carton of milk on the worktop and with angry fingers proceeded to tear it open. 'So, if that's all you came to tell me, you may as well leave.'

'That is not what I came for.' His tone had become sharp again. 'As I already told you, I have come to take you away from here.'

'Then you may as well leave anyway. I'm going nowhere.'

'Kindly don't waste my time, *habibiti*!' All at once he had stepped forward and grabbed her by the wrist, splashing milk all over the worktop as the carton slipped from her hand. 'Why must you argue with everything I say? Just for once, do as I tell you!'

'I will not do as you tell me! Why the hell should I? And I most certainly am not going anywhere with you!'

'Oh, yes, you are.' His voice was low, but the iron grip on her wrist had tightened. 'Either with or without a bag of your things, you will be leaving this villa within the next ten minutes and coming to my home to stay with me!'

'To stay with you?' What was this? An abduction? 'You must be out of your mind! What the devil do you take me for?'

'An incautious fool—that's what I take you for. And it is *you* who are out of your mind, staying alone in this house!'

'I'd be an incautious fool if I went with you! I'm much safer here, alone in the villa!'

As she'd struggled against him, he had simply pulled her closer, so that their two bodies were pressed hard against each other. 'You feel unsafe with me?' He smiled down at her wickedly. 'In what sense, pray, do you feel unsafe?'

There was no way she could answer him. Angela averted her eyes, her skin burning where he touched her, her senses jangling at his nearness.

'Are you afraid I might harm you? Perhaps beat you or lock you up?' With the subtlest of movements he drew her even closer. 'Tell me, fair Angela, is that what you fear?'

He knew damned fine it wasn't. Angrily, she shook her head.

'Then what is about me that you fear?' he insisted.

'I didn't say I feared anything.'

'You said I made you feel unsafe. What exactly did you mean, *habibiti*?'

'I didn't mean anything.' She tore her eyes away, so that he might not read the truth that was written there. For she did feel unsafe, she did feel afraid, and what scared her was this sense of vulnerability he awoke in her. It was as though she was no longer in charge of her own responses.

And still he was holding her. She could feel the warmth of him scorching against her own trembling flesh. Her eyes flickered back to his. She could not help it. Secretly she longed to drown in their depths.

'Is this what you feared?' His lips parted as he looked at her. Suddenly his free hand had slid to her waist.

Angela swallowed, unable to speak, her eyes drifting involuntarily to the wide sensuous mouth. And if there was a trace of fear in her heart at that moment, against the sudden surge of longing that overwhelmed her, it was tiny, of no importance.

The hand on her wrist slid possessively up her arm to grip her lightly by the shoulder. And, though she wanted him to kiss her, suddenly far more fiercely than she had ever wanted anything in her life, she was secretly certain that it wouldn't happen.

He was simply toying with her, trying to make a point. He was bound to stop short of anything so intimate.

Perhaps he read that in her eyes and saw it as a challenge. Or perhaps he had intended to kiss her from the start. He breathed something in Arabic, a sound as sweet as honey, and then he was gathering her into his arms and bending to cover her mouth with his.

Angela let out a little cry of pleasure as an unexpected pulse of warm excitement drove through her, making her heartbeat quicken and her skin flush hotly and her limbs feel as though they were rooted to the spot. Suddenly every nerve-end in her body was glowing, the blood pumping through her veins at twice its normal speed. And there was a dizzy sensation in her head, as though she were suddenly floating up in space.

His mouth was warm and masterful and demanding, striking sparks of desire against her senses, making her moan deep in her throat. And as one hand swept up to tangle with her hair, snatching it free from the band that held it back, his fingers driving against her sensitive scalp, sending hot and cold shivers to the soles of her feet, Angela was all at once quite startlingly aware of something she had perhaps always known in her heart.

Rashid al-Hazar was far and away the most desirable man she had ever known. And, what was more, she loved the carnal power he had over her. The way her senses throbbed. The way he made her head spin. No sensation she had ever known before had been quite so overpoweringly delicious.

He kissed her like a demon, as though he would possess her, his lips one moment feathering hers, soft and caressing, then precisely at the point where she became breathless with anticipation his mouth would come pressing down hard against hers, firm and demanding, making her soul ache.

And with each touch of his lips against her own she could feel him, like a demon, entering into her. And through the haze in her head she could sense that she was welcoming him.

But then, without warning, he was drawing away from her, and the lips that an atom ago had caused her to melt with pleasure were drawn into a hard and unforgiving line. Angela felt her heart freeze as in clipped tones he told her, 'You were right, *habibiti*. You have a great deal to fear. If this is the manner in which you feel free to comport yourself when you are here alone without your father to keep an eye on you, it is as well that I have come to take you away.'

The suddenness of the change in him was both brutal and shocking, and it induced an equally violent change in Angela. In an instant all the warmth within her had evaporated, to be replaced by a sense of unbridled indignation.

'What are you talking about—when my father's not here to keep an eye on me?' She pulled herself away from him and glared at him in fury. '*You're* the one who needs keeping an eye on!'

'*I?*' He raised black eyebrows. 'I am not his daughter. I am not the one who needs to be protected from herself.'

Why, the barefaced insolence of him! Swiftly Angela corrected him. 'The one who needs to be protected from *you*, you mean! You're the one who should be put in handcuffs!'

He smiled without humour. 'Did my hands abuse you? I was not aware of you trying to fight me off.'

'That's not the point!' But Angela felt herself colour. From the look in his eyes he knew she had enjoyed it.

Still, she stood her ground. 'I shouldn't have to fight you off! You shouldn't have touched me in the first place!'

Rashid shrugged eloquently. 'That is not how men are made—at least, not men who have red blood flowing through their veins. When a man sees an invitation in a woman's eyes he does not wait around for her to put that invitation into words.'

Damned rabid chauvinist! 'So, it was all my fault? I might have guessed that none of the blame would be yours!'

'Blame, you call it?' Unexpectedly he smiled. 'I would not use so pejorative a term for such a tiny lapse which, in the event, proved to be both pleasant and perfectly harmless.' Then he paused, his eyes narrowing. 'However, next time you may not be so lucky. Not all men, I warn you, are as self-disciplined as I am.'

'So that was a display of self-discipline, was it?' Angela's anger ran away with her tongue for a moment. Then she stopped short, aware that her words sounded like a challenge.

'Would you like to see what happens when I don't exercise self-discipline?' Just as she had expected, he had responded to the challenge.

As he took a step towards her, Angela took a step back. 'I most certainly do not!' She eyed him ferociously. 'I was simply pointing out that I would have been more impressed if you had refrained from kissing me altogether.'

Rashid smiled at her mockingly. 'I am not made of cardboard. Self-discipline is one thing, but self-denial is another. Why should I deny myself such fleeting carnal pleasures when they are obviously there for the taking?'

Angela swung away from him, seething with anger. 'I've had enough of this conversation. I'm going to bed!' Perhaps if she locked herself in her bedroom, he would renounce his misguided mission and go back home alone.

But Rashid al-Hazar was not so easily out-manoeuvred. Before she had taken barely two steps he was standing in front of her, blocking her path.

'The only purpose for which you are going to your room is to pack a bag. I have already told you you will be spending the night at my place.'

'I know what you've told me!' Angela glared at him. 'But I have no intention of doing any such thing!'

He was fast losing patience. His eyes were black and dangerous as he folded his arms across his chest. 'I'm beginning to grow weary of this argument,' he warned her. 'You're coming with me and that's all there is to it.'

'But why?' Angela could have wept from frustration. 'I'm perfectly happy staying here on my own. I'm not afraid, if that's what you're thinking.'

'You have no cause to be afraid—of burglars or molesters. This is a law-abiding country. But that is not the point.' His eyes drove through her. 'The point is that it is simply not acceptable for a nubile young woman to live on her own. Particularly,' he added with biting emphasis, 'when she is in the habit of entertaining male visitors.'

'Then you shouldn't have come, should you?' Angela accused him. 'You were the one who broke the rules!'

'I think you are forgetting...' He lifted one eyebrow. 'When I arrived you were expecting someone else. That was quite clear from the way you opened up the door.'

Angela glanced away. He was quite right; she had forgotten. She had been expecting Vince to drop in and see her.

Rashid's black eyes were watching her. 'Am I right?'

'It was only Vince. Just a friendly visit. All perfectly harmless. Nothing to get alarmed about.'

'Perhaps.' Rashid paused, his expression shuttered. 'And then again, perhaps not,' he added cryptically. 'Who's to know? And in such a situation you are unlikely to be given the benefit of the doubt.'

'By whom?' Angela demanded. 'You mean by you?'

'Not particularly by me. By anyone who's aware of your comings and goings.' He waved at the window. 'By your neighbours, for example. Neighbours see a great deal from behind their curtains.'

'Well, I don't give a damn what the neighbours see! Nor do I care what sordid conclusions they wish to come to! No one's going to stop me from having an innocent visit from a workmate who just happens to be a man!'

'That's where you're wrong.' He dropped his hands to his sides and let out a sigh of exasperation. '*I'm* going to stop you, and I'm going to stop you right now. You see, I *do* give a damn what the neighbours might say.'

'And why should you care? What business is it of yours?'

'I care because I'm your employer. Your bad reputation reflects badly on me.'

'So, now I have a bad reputation?'

'You will have soon if you carry on this way.'

'You mean I'm not allowed to have any male visitors or the whole neighbourhood will believe I'm running some kind of brothel?' Angela was shaking now, she felt so insulted and angry.

Rashid shook his head calmly. 'No need to exaggerate.' Then he sighed and smiled a lopsided smile. 'Look, you can have all the visitors you like, including Vince, since his company appears to be so important to you . . . just as soon as you move into my place. There will be no problem there because you will be chaperoned.'

'Chaperoned? By you, you mean? I'm sorry, but I don't fancy you as my chaperon, breathing down the back of my neck all the time!'

'Don't worry about that. Acting as your chaperon is not numbered among the duties I feel obliged to perform for you. But in my house there are many servants—and my sister lives there—so there will be plenty of chaperons available.'

'Your sister?' Angela blinked. For some strange reason it surprised her that Rashid should have a sister—or any family at all, come to that. She had imagined him existing in a state of splendid isolation.

He read her mind. 'I have three sisters, two of whom are married, and three brothers, all younger than myself.' As she continued to stare at him, he elaborated with amusement, 'Believe it or not, I also have a mother and a father. All perfectly regular. All perfectly normal.'

He was still standing in front of her, blocking her exit from the kitchen, but he had dropped his previous belligerent pose. Perhaps this was the moment to try a little negotiation, Angela decided, mentally crossing her fingers. She fixed a smile on her face and looked up at him appealingly. 'Listen . . .' she began. 'About this business of male visitors . . .'

'Yes?' he enquired with the lift of one eyebrow.

'Well, it seems to me there's an easy solution . . .'

'Tell me about it,' he invited.

Angela took a deep breath. 'All I have to do is not have any visitors until my father comes back from hospital. Then no one will have any cause to think anything bad.' She smiled at him sweetly. 'It's the perfect solution.'

For a long moment Rashid looked down into her eyes. Then he shook his head slowly. 'Sorry, but that won't do.'

Anger flared within her. He was being unreasonable. 'Why ever not?' Angela demanded irritably.

'I thought I'd already told you...' His tone was irritated, too. 'It simply is not acceptable in this country that a young woman like yourself should live on her own.'

'Well, I think that's ridiculous! I live on my own in London! Nobody thinks there's anything strange about it there!'

His answer was predictable. 'Then go back to London. That is what I have been advising you to do all along.'

'I don't want your advice. And I'm not going with you.' Angela folded her arms across her chest. 'Don't think you can just snap your fingers at me and I'll do what you tell me!'

'I'll give you one more chance. I'll count up to ten.' He snapped his fingers to annoy her. 'Go and pack a bag and let's be on our way.'

Angela thrust her chin at him. 'You can count up to a thousand. I haven't the slightest intention of budging from here.'

Rashid started counting. 'One...' he began.

'You're wasting your time.'

'Two...' he carried on.

'You realise this is ridiculous? You're making a fuss over nothing.'

He ignored her totally. 'Four...' he counted softly.

What was going to happen when he finally reached ten? Suddenly Angela's heart was beating faster. She cast a glance past him at the kitchen door. If she could dart past him and make it to her room, she could lock herself in and then she'd be safe.

But she would never make it. She knew that for certain. He would have caught her before she was even halfway across the kitchen.

As he counted to seven, Angela bit her lip. 'Let's wait till we can speak to MacLeish about this. As you probably know, he's over in Bahrain for a few days—but as soon as he gets back I'll go and talk to him and see what he has to say on the subject. As a long-standing resident of this country, I'm sure he's in a position to give me reliable advice.'

She might as well have spoken to the wind. Rashid murmured, 'Ten...' and took a step towards her. 'It looks as though you'll be leaving without any baggage,' he observed grimly.

'I keep telling you, I'm not going anywhere with you!' Stubbornly Angela stood her ground, though she could sense exactly what his next move was going to be.

He stepped towards her, making her blood leap, and laid one hand upon her arm. 'Will you come without a fuss or do I have to carry you? I confess I would prefer the former solution.'

As Angela glared into his face, a sudden thought occurred to her. Perhaps she could yet win this battle of wills. 'Just imagine,' she put to him, 'what the neighbours would think if you were to carry me out of here kicking and screaming. That would give them something to talk about! Sheikh Rashid al-Hazar kidnapping a young English girl!'

Her threat merely amused him. 'You are absolutely right. Such a scene would give them something to talk about for days. No doubt they would have an absolute field-day speculating on what you might have done to merit such treatment.' As she scowled at his response, he smilingly assured her, 'Take my word that such a scene would merely rebound on you. Unless you care to invite scandal, I would not advise it.'

Though it was galling, Angela sensed he was probably right. As a man and a sheikh he would be above social criticisms. She, as a female, was much more vulnerable—and she had no desire to create a scandal. This, after all, was her father's home and he would have to go on living here long after she was gone.

For the moment she was beaten. 'OK, I'll come quietly.' With an angry gesture she pushed his hand away. 'But this is only until MacLeish gets back. I intend to speak to him and hear what he has to say.'

Rashid shrugged indifferently. 'Speak to him if you like. Once he's thought properly about the issue, I'm sure he'll agree with me. In fact, he'll probably kick himself for not having done something about it sooner.'

Then, as she scowled up at him, he added crisply, 'Surely you don't believe that, if there were any other way, I would inflict upon myself and my household such disagreeable company as yours? Believe me, the arrangement appeals to me no more than it does to you.'

As she flinched a little at the insult, he stood aside and bade her pass. 'Since you've decided to be reasonable, after all, I'll give you five minutes to pack a bag. But only five minutes. Not a second more.'

Through in her bedroom, rigid with fury, Angela flung some bare essentials into a bag—a nightdress, some toiletries and a couple of changes of clothes—then pulled off her kaftan and pulled on a T-shirt and skirt.

He needn't worry, she was thinking hotly, she wouldn't be inflicting her disagreeable company on him or his household for a moment longer than was necessary!

For she could just imagine what it was going to be like having to eat and sleep under the same roof as him. In everyday life the man was impossible—autocratic and arrogant and overbearing. Heaven knew what he would be like in the privacy of his own home! He probably ruled the place as though it were some private little kingdom, surrounded by brow-beaten, forelock-tugging servants, all crawling on their knees to do his bidding. Even his poor sister was probably kept locked in her room!

With a shiver of distaste Angela zipped up her bag. MacLeish was due back the day after tomorrow. She would manage to endure her taste of hell until then.

Rashid was waiting for her impatiently in the hall when she emerged with her bag slung over her shoulder. 'I'll take that.' He almost snatched it from her, then proceeded to lead her towards the front door.

Outside, the night air was still and balmy. A huge crescent moon hung low in the sky. And beyond the garden wall, waiting to whisk her off to purgatory, stood Rashid's long white gleaming Cadillac.

He dropped her bag into the cavernous boot, then marched round to open up the passenger door for her. *'T'fuddli,'* he invited. 'Kindly get in.'

Angela would never forget that drive across Jahira and her first sight of the place that Rashid called home.

Neither of them spoke. Angela was too angry, and Rashid, she presumed, had his own bad-tempered reasons. He switched on some music as they headed towards the open desert, passing only a handful of other cars on the way, skirting the occasional sleeping village shielded from curious eyes by high sandstone walls.

Then, just as Angela was starting to wonder where the devil he was taking her, they turned a corner and there before them, ablaze with a thousand lights in the darkness, stood a magnificent, sprawling Arabian palace.

Angela let out a gasp of wonder at the sight of it. 'Is this where you live?' It was breathtakingly beautiful.

Rashid turned to smile at her as they drove through the main gates into a courtyard full of palm trees, with a fountain playing. 'Do you like it?' he enquired, watching her face.

'It's like something out of a fairy-tale!' Angela laughed in response, quite unable to suppress her delight. 'I've never seen anything like it in my life!'

'I thought it would appeal to you.' His eyes were soft as he watched her. 'When I was a child I thought it was magical. I'm afraid I've come to take it a little for granted over the years.'

'Oh, I could never do that!' Angela gazed about her wonderingly as Rashid reached across her to open up her door. 'I could live here all my life and never cease to be enchanted!'

What a stupid thing to say! What on earth had possessed her? Bright colour suddenly flared in Angela's cheeks as a rush of embarrassment went washing through her. And, to add to her confusion, at that very same moment, as Rashid withdrew his hand after opening up her door for her, his arm brushed lightly against her breasts.

At the touch of him a flare of excitement shot through her, burning her cheeks an even brighter crimson, causing her heart to break into a gallop. Her eyes fixed to the paving stones, she stumbled out into the courtyard. What the devil was happening to her? She was behaving like an idiot!

'Come this way. Follow me!'

Apparently oblivious of her odd behaviour, Rashid had retrieved her bag from the boot and was leading her now up some steps to the main entrance—through a high ornate doorway, then into a huge tiled hall, splendidly lit with hanging brass lanterns, and with bright Persian rugs strewn across the floor.

Angela suppressed another admiring gasp. It was even more beautiful inside than out!

'I'm afraid at this late hour all the servants are in bed.' Rashid paused beneath an archway that led to a wide corridor. 'So, I shall have to show you to your room myself.'

Angela shrugged, composing her features, disciplining herself to act cool and indifferent. There had been enough childish enthusiasm and immature gaffes. It was time she salvaged what was left of her dignity.

'That's fine,' she answered, not quite meeting his gaze. The less she said, the better, she decided.

On swift strides he led her down the corridor, then up a huge curved staircase and down yet another passageway to a quiet, tucked-away corner of the vast house.

At last he stopped outside an ornately gilded door, pushed it open, stood aside, and told her, 'This is your room. It has its own private bathroom. I trust you'll find everything you need.' Then he laid her bag down and informed her, 'My sister's room is just next door.'

'I see; this is the women's quarters?' She shot him a look. 'It struck me as being a little remote.'

She said it to annoy him, to redress the balance between them. She had been too full of admiration, too ready with her compliments, and it was simply intended as a gesture to put him in his place.

But he thwarted her by smiling. 'If you would prefer to sleep with me, you are more than welcome, *habibiti*.' He raised one black eyebrow and looked straight into her eyes. 'I have a large and very welcoming bed.'

The open invitation sent a prickle down Angela's spine, a prickle that she pretended to herself was horror. She stepped past him swiftly into the room. 'No, thank you. I prefer to sleep next door to your sister.'

'A wise decision.' He smiled again, wickedly. 'The alternative option undoubtedly has its merits, but I doubt that either of us would get much sleep.' He bowed a mocking bow. 'Goodnight, *habibiti*.' Then, as she started to close the door, he intercepted. 'You'd better give me the keys to your car. I'll get someone to pick it up first thing in the morning.'

Angela fished for her car-keys and virtually threw them at him. But he simply smiled. 'Sleep well, fair Angela. I look forward to seeing you in the morning.'

Angela slammed the door shut. 'Damn him!' she muttered. 'Damn him for bringing me here! Damn him for existing!'

Still throbbing with anger, she washed and changed in the sumptuous bathroom, with its gilded wash-basin and solid gold taps, then climbed into the vast silk-covered bed. But, in spite of her carefully fuelled indignation, it was an effort to keep her mind from straying to the image of Rashid, somewhere along those corridors, lying in his own 'very welcoming' bed—and even more of an effort to stop her spine from tingling each time she remembered how it had felt when he had kissed her.

She turned over impatiently and scowled into the darkness and tried to rationalise away these dangerous thoughts. There was a perfectly simple explanation for this silly attraction she felt for him. He was different. He was exotic. He was stunningly handsome. And all these factors combined together to make him seem irresistibly exciting.

But the real truth was—if Angela examined the facts carefully—that he was nothing but an arrogant, overbearing autocrat, the last sort of man any sane woman should get involved with.

And I am most definitely quite sane, Angela reminded herself sharply.

So the solution was simple. She must continue to try to avoid him. That way there would be no danger of temptation overcoming reason.

She drifted off to sleep with a promise on her lips. Her stay at the palace would be brief.

And solitary.

CHAPTER FIVE

The following day, a day earlier than expected, Angela had a chance to speak to MacLeish.

'He's on the phone from Bahrain. I told him you wanted a word with him,' Lalitha told her, beckoning her into her office.

Angela offered a mild protest. 'That's very good of you, but it's really not necessary. I can speak to him tomorrow when he gets back.'

But Lalitha shook her head and handed her the receiver. 'I think you ought to speak to him now.'

Angela soon found out why.

'I understand you've got something you want to ask me.' MacLeish queried in his soft Scottish accent. 'Well, you'd better fire away. This'll be your last chance to speak to me for a few weeks, I'm afraid. As soon as I'm finished here I'm flying off to the States.'

The significance of that revelation failed to strike Angela immediately, as she launched into an impassioned protest about her removal to Rashid's palace. 'Don't you agree?' she finished emotionally. 'It's utterly ridiculous!'

There was a momentary pause, then at last MacLeish answered her. 'I'm afraid it's not. Sheikh Rashid is right, and I ought to have thought of it myself. Just you stay where you are until your father's out of hospital. And, if you have any other problems, consult Sheikh Rashid. He'll be running things while I'm away.'

Angela handed back the phone, feeling stunned and speechless. Not only was she to be stuck indefinitely at the palace, but it looked as though she was also about to plagued by Rashid's more or less constant presence at the office. Things were going from bad to worse!

And how right she was! The very next day a memo was circulated, announcing that during the editor's absence Sheikh Rashid would be presiding over the daily editorial meeting. He really would be breathing down everyone's neck!

Editorial meetings were normally held in MacLeish's office, in an atmosphere that was businesslike but informal. But, on the memo's instructions, that evening at six Angela and the half-dozen other reporters gathered with their notepads in the sumptuous boardroom to await Sheikh Rashid's arrival.

'Trust him to be late,' Angela observed in a caustic tone to Sharma, the paper's business affairs reporter, who was seated at her side round the huge mahogany table.

But, typically, Sharma smiled back with quiet tolerance. 'Sheikh Rashid is a very busy man. We can't really complain if he's a few minutes late.'

They were so damned loyal to him—the entire *News* staff! Angela thought to herself with irritation. Couldn't they see he was a selfish, self-seeking autocrat?

She glanced back at Sharma. 'If you ask me, we could have managed perfectly well without him. We really don't need him sticking his nose in.'

It was at that precise moment that Rashid swept into the room, causing a rustle of attention as all eyes turned towards him. And, as his gaze for an instant brushed Angela's face, she wondered if he had overheard her comment.

Too bad if he had! she thought, watching him beneath her lashes. That happened to be her opinion and she wasn't afraid to express it.

He had swept to the head of the table and seated himself with a flourish. 'Good evening, gentlemen. Let's get started!' Then he paused and with a slow smile let his gaze drift to Angela. 'Forgive me. A small correction. Good evening, lady and gentlemen. Force of habit, I'm afraid.'

As a polite ripple of laughter drifted round the table, he kept his gaze fixed on Angela's strictly impassive face. 'Allow me to welcome you to our midst. It's always a pleasure to have a lady present, especially one as fair and as decorative as yourself.'

Angela felt her lips compress together with irritation. What a typically chauvinistic remark! 'Thank you,' she answered, meeting his gaze without flinching. 'However, I trust my contribution to the proceedings will prove to be more than purely decorative.'

As she spoke she was aware of a silent gasp of astonishment coming from her colleagues on either side of her. Clearly, none of them had ever heard their managing director addressed in so bold a manner before.

Rashid himself betrayed no reaction, other than the faintly amused lifting of one eyebrow. He continued to hold her gaze for a moment, then turned his attention to the others. 'Very well, then. Shall we begin?'

The meeting proceeded then without further ado, and in spite of herself Angela found herself admiring the smooth masterful way in which Rashid handled it. The *Jahira News* might be only a hobby to him, but it was clearly a hobby that he took very seriously.

He appeared to be quite impressively well-acquainted with every detail of the editorial running of the paper. As the reporters discussed the pieces they were working on, he listened with attention, interrupting now and then to make some shrewd, incisive comment. Yet there was nothing dictatorial about his style. Rather he appeared to function as the leader of a team.

Not his usual style at all, Angela thought with a touch of cynicism, frankly amazed at his ability to control his natural tendency to bully. But perhaps, she decided, it's just women he likes to tread on. For there was certainly no hint of his usual rough arrogance in his treatment of the reporters.

Angela continued to watch him, oddly mesmerised by this unfamiliar display of charm and subtlety. In this new mood the harsh lines of his features had relaxed, the wide mouth captivatingly sensual, the dark brow unfurrowed, the dark eyes

touched with humour. Like this, there was a warmth
to him she had glimpsed only once before—that
time in his office when she had told him about her
mother.

Was it real or was it just an act? she wondered.
'And now to the opening of the new National
Theatre.' As he said it, he pushed back the white
kaffiyeh to expose a glimpse of jet-black sideburn.
'I take it you'll be doing a piece on that, Angela?'

Angela blinked at the question. 'I beg your
pardon?' For her mind hadn't really been on what
he was saying, but engaged in the contemplation
of that glossy black sideburn.

Was the hair beneath the *kaffiyeh* as glossy and
as black? Was it long? Was it short? Was it curly?
Was it straight?

'The National Theatre,' he repeated a trifle impatiently, toying with the pencil he held between
his long brown fingers. 'You will, I assume, be
doing an article?'

Frankly appalled at herself as his eyes bored into
her, Angela quickly pulled herself together. 'I expect
so,' she responded, despising her own lack of authority. But the truth was that it hadn't occurred to
her to do an article. She cleared her throat and
straightened her shoulders. 'Was there any particular angle you thought I ought to cover?'

He smiled at that, but it was a smile that was
faintly abrasive. 'I'm surprised I have to tell you.
A young woman like yourself, who sees herself as
the champion of her sisters . . . I expected you to be
banging on your desk and demanding an interview

with the theatre's architect.' He paused. 'I take it you are aware of this person's identity.'

To her dismay, Angela was obliged to shake her head. 'I'm afraid I don't. I know the firm of architects who designed the theatre is French, but I don't know the name of the man who headed the design team.'

Rashid's smile grew more abrasive. 'The man who headed the design team was a woman. A certain Madame Catherine Bouquet.'

Angela could have kicked herself. She felt her cheeks flush. 'Oh,' she mumbled, feeling an absolute fool.

'Madame Bouquet will be in Jahira for the opening of the theatre. I suggest you contact the Press office to arrange an interview—that is, of course, if the subject matter interests you.' He flicked her a look and sat back in his seat, balancing his pencil between the tips of his index fingers. 'If you prefer to fill your page with knitting patterns and recipes, it's really all the same to me.'

He smiled as he said it, inviting a titter of amusement from the other reporters gathered round the table. Angela bit her lip, secretly writhing beneath his mockery. He was making a fool both of her and of her women's page. His opposition to the project was evidently still alive and thriving.

Angela spoke through the laughter, her tone controlled and even. 'I shall most certainly be doing an interview,' she told him. 'Thank you for the information.'

He smiled. 'Don't mention it. That's what I'm here for.' Then he turned to the others. 'Any other business?'

The meeting was adjourned shortly after that. Without looking at him, Angela gathered up her pad and pencil and, along with the others, began to head for the door. But she was stopped halfway.

'If you don't mind, Angela, I'd like a word with you in private.'

Angela's heart sank. So, she was in for more abuse. What other reason could he have for singling her out?

As the door closed behind the other reporters, she turned, arms folded protectively across her chest. 'Yes?' she enquired politely. And waited.

He was still seated in his place at the head of the table, long fingers toying idly with his pencil. He waved at one of the chairs next to his own. 'Make yourself comfortable. Take a seat.'

So, he was planning on inflicting an extended torture. Her heart sank even further as, with great reluctance, she took the chair furthest away from him that politeness allowed. But it was still far too close. His nearness was oppressive.

And suddenly, for some reason, her mouth had gone dry. Apprehension, she told herself. I'm in no mood for a fight.

He leaned back in his seat and adjusted his *kaffiyeh*, flicking it back over his shoulders with an elegant gesture, revealing once again that glimpse of glossy sideburn.

Then he smiled unexpectedly. 'I ought to tell you I enjoyed that article of yours in the women's page last week. The one on infertility and its treatment. It was very well-researched and sensitively written.'

Was this praise she was hearing? Angela couldn't believe it. She blinked at him as though he had just grown two heads.

'I'm glad you liked it.' And the silly thing was she meant it. 'I was very lucky in having Dr Shawki available to interview. As a specialist in that field, he gave me a great deal of help.'

'It was a well-written article. You got the facts across clearly. When it comes to technical subjects like that journalists all too often get themselves tied up in knots.'

'But I'm a professional, as I've already told you. It's my job to get complex issues across in such a way that the layman will understand them.'

If she was shrugging off his compliments as though they didn't mean a thing to her, that was simply because she didn't know how else to react. He had a habit of throwing her off balance, but this time he had succeeded in disorientating her totally. Compliments and praise were the very last things she'd been expecting!

He continued to smile at her. 'You did a good job. If you keep up that sort of standard we may yet see eye to eye.'

Frankly, Angela doubted it, and suddenly she was angry at this somewhat belated display of approval. Was she expected to wag her tail like a puppy just because he'd deigned to pat her on the head?

Well, she would do no such thing. On the contrary, she would tell him precisely what was in her mind!

Sitting up straight, she looked him in the eye. 'What a pity you couldn't have mentioned this when the other reporters were around, instead of deliberately making a fool of me over that business of the National Theatre architect.'

If he was surprised by her reaction, he did not show it. He tapped the pencil lightly on the table top and met her gaze with narrowed dark eyes. 'You were the one who was at fault, I would suggest. You ought to have been aware of Madame Bouquet's identity.'

'In theory, you're right.' Angela looked back at him unblinkingly. 'It's a journalist's job to know these things. But I've only been doing this job for a couple of weeks—scarcely long enough to build up any kind of information network. And I happen to be starting from scratch, remember. I haven't even inherited any sort of network from anyone else.'

'I don't deny that. And normally I would agree with you. In fact, that is the reason I gave you the information.' He paused and fixed her with eyes that had turned to daggers. 'But I seem to remember, when I arrived to take the meeting, overhearing you remark that my presence here was superfluous, that you could have managed perfectly well without me...'

So, he had heard her, after all. Angela blushed to her hair roots.

'Let's just say I decided to teach you a lesson.'

And a humiliatingly public lesson at that! Angela clenched her jaw. 'I see,' she responded. If he was waiting for an apology, he would wait forever.

But he seemed uninterested in her apologies, or the lack of them. He sat back in his seat again. 'But that's not why I wanted to talk to you. What I was intending to ask you was if you'd settled in OK at the palace?'

Such gallant concern after she had been virtually kidnapped! She slid him a cool look. 'I'm quite comfortable, thank you.'

'I'm glad to hear it.' He sounded amused by her displeasure. 'Since you are likely to be there for some little time yet, I would hate to think that you might have any complaints. Unfortunately, we seem to have missed each other at mealtimes. I hope you don't mind too much eating alone?'

'Not in the slightest.' She had missed him on purpose, having ascertained from the kitchen staff at what times he generally took his meals.

Then, as a thought occurred to her, she cast him a curious glance. 'I haven't seen anything of your sister, either. Doesn't she ever leave her room?'

'From time to time.' He smiled with superior amusement. 'She's been rather busy lately, I believe.'

Angela arched a cynical eyebrow. 'Busy, you say? And what keeps her so occupied that she never shows her face? Is she cloistered in there, embroidering her trousseau or enjoying some such other exciting pursuit that Arab princes allow their sisters to get up to?'

It was at that moment that there was a light tap on the door. Then Lalitha stuck her head round, her expression apologetic. 'Excuse me, sir. There's an urgent call for you. Would you like to take it here?'

'I'll take it in a moment. Right now I'm in a meeting.' His tone was brusque. He did not glance at his secretary, but kept his gaze fixed unblinkingly on Angela.

With a deferential nod Lalitha retreated, and suddenly Angela could feel her blood boil. No wonder Lalitha at times seemed upset. Rashid treated her abominably—just as he no doubt treated his sister, and every other woman he encountered!

She rose to her feet, bristling with disapproval. 'If that's all, sir, I'll go now. I have work to do.'

He did not answer for a moment, just looked her up and down, minutely, unhurriedly, as though she were a contender in some cattle-market beauty contest. She could feel his eyes stripping away her light cotton dress and caressing the firm young flesh beneath.

Then he smiled at her lazily and waved one hand dismissively. 'Yes, you may go. I've finished with you for the moment.'

There was no escaping daily contact with Rashid. At the palace it was relatively easy to avoid him, for he seemed to spend very little time at home—

scarcely surprising, considering that he was doing two jobs! But in the office it was impossible to stay out of his way.

In MacLeish's absence he had adopted the habit of dropping in at the *News* office a couple of times a day—and *always*, it seemed to Angela, when she was around.

He would come striding in, head-dress flying, electrifying the atmosphere just by his presence, and proceed to take charge as naturally as breathing. And that was Angela's cue to rivet her eyes to her typewriter and pray that she would not be singled out for special attention.

Sometimes she was and sometimes she wasn't. Occasionally, he would pounce on her unexpectedly, sometimes to check up on her: 'That piece you're doing on women's education in Jahira...I'd like to take a look at it before you go any further. Just to make sure you've got the right sort of approach.'

At other times he would pretend he was trying to be helpful: 'I suggest you have a word with the Lebanese Ambassador's wife about that cookery series you're running. I'm sure she'd be happy to share a few recipes.'

But whenever she sensed him pause by her desk or felt his eyes swivel towards her during the editorial meeting, Angela was instantly on her guard. He was out to trip her up, to make a fool of her, to make her appear brash and unfit for the job.

But, since that first time, he had never caught her out. And he never would. Angela had sworn it.

She had smiled to herself that day in his office when he had handed back her article on women's education with the no doubt reluctant observation, 'Well, I can't see anything to complain about in that. I would say you've struck a very fair balance between the progressive and the more traditional schools of thought.'

'Thank you,' she had answered, her tone touched with irony. 'So kind of you to let me know that you approve.'

'Don't worry, I'll also let you know when I don't.' Black dagger eyes had met hers across the desk-top. 'You're still very much on trial here, remember. Don't let a couple of good articles go to your head.'

Rashid's eyes had held hers. Just one wrong move, they were saying, and you'll to be out on your ear before you know what's happening!

Irked, she'd glared back at him. 'I wouldn't dream of it. I'm well aware of how ecstatic you are about having me here.'

He had smiled at that. 'I'm glad we understand each other. It makes for a more realistic working relationship. I would hate for you to get the wrong idea and start thinking that you really belonged.'

The observation had stung, for she had indeed been starting to feel that. With each day that passed she felt more and more at home. But she had regarded him impassively as she'd answered, 'Don't worry, I haven't carved my name in my desk.'

Damn him! she had thought later. How he enjoyed flexing his muscles and constantly reminding her how much at his mercy she was!

And it had suddenly struck her that she ought to be prepared, when her father was eventually released from hospital, to discover that her Residence Permit had been cancelled. It had occurred to her before that more than likely Rashid had allowed her permit to go through out of some fleeting, uncharacteristic humanitarian impulse, so that she could be close to her father during his illness. As soon as the situation returned to normal, she had a nasty suspicion, her permit would be revoked.

Unless, she told herself with unflinching determination, I can prove to him that I really am the right woman for the job. And she was on the right track. Instinctively, she sensed it. So far he had been reluctantly impressed by her work. She must continue that way and beware of making slips.

For, in spite of the fact that, while MacLeish was away, Rashid's constant presence at the office was a torment, with each day that passed she loved the job more and her confidence in her ability to handle it was growing. With a little more time, she was increasingly hopeful, she could inspire equal confidence in Sheikh Rashid.

It was the following week, as she was leaving the office one evening, that just as she was heading down the corridor towards the exit Sheikh Rashid's office door suddenly burst open and Lalitha came rushing out of it in tears.

'Hey, what's the matter?' Angela hurried up to her. 'What on earth has he done to you now?'

Lalitha shook her head, evidently too upset to answer. The tears were pouring down her cheeks.

'Is there anything I can do?' Angela put her arm around her, but Lalitha shook her head again.

'Thank you, no,' she managed to stutter. Then she drew away from Angela's embrace and began to hurry in the direction of her own office. 'I'd like to be on my own for a moment.'

'Of course, of course. I understand. But just say the word if I can do anything at all.'

She watched with a frown as the girl moved away, her thin shoulders beneath her sari still shaking with emotion. And suddenly she was filled with an all-consuming anger against the cause of poor Lalitha's distress.

How dared he treat the poor girl with such insensitivity? Did he think that just because he was who he was he had a right to get away with it?

Well, he was wrong! she vowed, her eyes narrowing in sudden resolve, as she glared along the corridor towards his still-open doorway. Even if no one else had the courage to speak up to him, she wasn't afraid to give him a piece of her mind!

She marched along the corridor on legs stiff with outrage, and took a deep breath as she reached the open door. Then, heart thumping, she took a step inside and cleared her throat to catch his attention.

He had been leaning over some paperwork that was spread out across his desk, and he frowned now, quite evidently displeased at the interruption. 'Yes?' His tone was sharp. 'What can I do for you?'

Angela felt her outrage bubble over. He was so damned imperious, so unfeeling, so arrogant. That was probably precisely the same tone of voice that he had used to upset Lalitha. But she, unlike Lalitha, was not so easily put out.

She clenched her fists and looked straight at him. 'There's nothing you can do for me. I'm here to do something for you . . . To tell you precisely what I think of you!'

As she hesitated for a milli-second, one black eyebrow lifted. But, before he had time to interrupt her, Angela continued without a falter, 'I think you're the most unspeakable man I've ever met. A bully, a tyrant, a hateful monster. You think you can treat people any way you want and nobody's going to say a word to you! Well, I think it's high time that somebody did. I think it's time that somebody finally told you that there's nothing smart or particularly admirable about abusing your position of privilege the way that you do!'

He had sat back in his chair, his expression unreadable. 'I take it,' he enquired in a low voice, 'that that somebody is you.'

'Damned right it is!'

She stood quivering as she glared at him, aware in one semi-stunned corner of her brain that she had expressed herself rather more vehemently than she had intended. But she felt no regrets, though she knew she had blown it. He would never allow her to keep her job now.

As he continued to watch her, black eyes shuttered, she decided with a kind of nihilistic abandon that she might as well go out with a bang as with a whimper. She threw back her head and went on to inform him, 'You keep reminding me that you don't want me working for you . . . Well, let me tell you, I can't honestly say that I'm terribly keen about working for you, either! So, you can keep your job. I really don't care!'

Then she turned on her heel, her heart racing like a fire engine, and went stalking, stiff-legged, out of the door.

CHAPTER SIX

LATER, once she had calmed down, Angela squirmed with horror to recall the manner in which she had exploded at Rashid. The things she'd said! The insults she'd hurled at him! She must have been completely out of her mind!

Not that she regretted having stood up for Lalitha. That had been the right thing to do. But why couldn't she have done it in a controlled and rational fashion, as she would have done had she been dealing with any other man?

The trouble was, she was compelled to recognise, she found it virtually impossible to control her emotions where the unutterable Rashid was concerned. He didn't simply annoy her as others sometimes annoyed her; he infuriated her beyond all reason. He didn't just irk her or make her impatient or give her a proverbial pain in the neck. He incensed her to the point where she could not see straight. The mere sight of him seemed to set her emotions bubbling.

She felt deeply troubled by this realisation. It really wasn't like her in the slightest. No one had ever affected her this way, and it was a highly dangerous situation. For when she was around Rashid, she was starting to realise, even *she* couldn't be sure of what she might do next!

She sighed to herself. Bad chemistry, she decided. They were like a cat and a dog. They just weren't meant to mix.

And there was something else that troubled her about that episode. For since the evening of her outburst she hadn't set eyes on Lalitha again.

'She's gone back to India,' her colleague Sharma told her. 'Some problem in her family, I understand. She had to leave very unexpectedly.'

Angela felt her stomach squeeze with anxiety. Had Rashid upset the girl so badly that she'd gone flying back home to her family? And was it partly her fault? she wondered guiltily. Had her outburst only made the situation worse?

She frowned at Sharma. 'She will be back, though? As far as you know, she's not staying away forever?'

'I shouldn't think so.' Sharma laughed. 'They've got a temporary girl coming to fill in while she's gone, but this office couldn't run for long without Lalitha!'

That had been precisely Angela's impression, and yet Rashid treated her as though she were worthless. Again, just at the thought of him, Angela could feel her blood boil.

But over the next couple of days she was at least spared the upleasantness of having to come face to face with Rashid again. For a change, fate was kind and she was out on assignments when he made his visits to the office. She even had the good fortune to miss the editorial meetings.

And then came the weekend and she knew she could breathe easily. He spent little time at the palace at weekends, seeming to prefer working overtime at the Al-Hazar Tower.

She put up a prayer of heartfelt thanks. Eventually, she knew, she would have to confront him and pay the price of her insubordination. But it was definitely not something she was looking forward to.

After a morning spent visiting her father at the hospital—he was looking much better, actually sitting up in bed!—she returned to the palace and made herself some lunch, then stretched out on a sofa to flick through a magazine.

But somehow she couldn't settle. She felt distracted and fidgety. And, to add to her discomfort, the usually cool palace felt uncomfortably hot and sticky today. She decided to step outdoors for a moment.

Outside, of course, it was even hotter, but there was a trickle of a breeze blowing up from the bay. I'll explore the gardens, Angela decided. That was one part of her prison she had not yet investigated.

The gardens were nothing like an English garden, more a series of walled courtyards leading into one another, strung out like a necklace of flourishing greenery in the midst of the parched and barren desert. And as she strolled about, admiring the fountains and the flower-beds, she passed the time of day with some of the gardeners who tended them.

'Sabah il-kheer!' Good day, she greeted them.

'*Sabah i-noor,*' they responded politely.

Taking the path that skirted the side of the house, she was about to move on to the next little courtyard when her eye was caught by a man in blue jeans crouching with a spanner over the big outdoor motor that powered the palace's air-conditioning system. She was able to recognise what it was, for there was a similar, smaller contraption at her father's villa.

So that was why it had been so hot indoors! Something had gone wrong with the air-conditioning. Thank heavens that someone had been sent for to fix it!

The man had his back to her, so he probably hadn't even noticed her, but for politeness' sake she offered him a greeting.

'*Sabah il-kheer,*' she murmured without pausing.

But when the answer came back, 'Good afternoon, *habibiti,*' she spun round, startled, in her tracks.

He had turned now to look at her, amusement dancing in his eyes, and Angela felt her heart leap to her throat. He looked so startlingly different in grubby jeans and T-shirt, and yet so achingly handsome that she could scarcely speak.

'What on earth are you doing?' she finally managed to squeak.

'Fixing the AC. There was a problem with the motor.' He threw down the spanner. 'Hand me that rag.'

Angela was trying her hardest to pull herself together. She glanced around her bewilderedly for a moment, then, as he pointed, she noticed the tool-box inches from her feet. She snatched up the rag that was lying on top of it and handed it to Rashid as he reached out towards her.

'But why are *you* fixing it?' she enquired in confusion. 'And why on earth are you dressed like that?'

Rashid laughed as he wiped his oily hands on the rag, then slowly he stood up and tossed the rag aside. 'How should I dress?' he enquired, watching her. 'I think a *dishdasha* and *kaffiyeh* would be somewhat impractical attire for a messy job like this.'

'But you never dress like this!' Angela couldn't keep her eyes off him. The close-fitting T-shirt and narrow jeans showed off his lean powerful form to perfection. She had guessed at the muscularity of those copper-skinned arms, sprinkled, she could see now, with fine black hairs, and she had imagined the taut hard power of his thighs, the leanness of his hips, the breadth of his shoulders. But it was a shock to be faced with the vibrant reality.

'I didn't even recognise you!' she burbled foolishly. It was the first time she had even seen him with his head uncovered, and what a glorious thick head of glossy black hair he had!

'I often dress like this.' There was amusement in his tone. 'At home and, of course, when I'm abroad. I can't see why you should be so amazed.'

'But you look so different!'

'Well, I'm not, I assure you. Underneath all this...' he deliberately caught her eye '... I'm exactly the same hateful monster as before. The same old bully. The same old tyrant.'

Angela felt herself blanch to hear her insults repeated. Had she really said those things? As she stood here with him now they seemed oddly out of place.

But to her surprise and great relief he didn't pursue the subject. Instead, he turned away and made a quick check of the motor. 'That ought to have fixed it.' He adjusted a gauge. 'Let's go back inside and see if it's working.'

As he bent to gather up the tool-box at her feet, Angela glanced down at the jet-black hair—a little longer than she had imagined, curling softly against the back of his neck. 'You still haven't answered my question,' she put to him, her heart leaping a little as black eyes looked up at her. 'Why did you have to fix the air-conditioning yourself? Couldn't you get a mechanic to come and do it?'

'Sure, I could.' He straightened sinuously, picking up the heavy tool-box as though it were a matchbox. 'But I enjoy doing these little jobs myself. I like working with my hands whenever I get the chance. It makes a refreshing change from sitting behind a desk.'

Angela regarded him with curious narrowed eyes. It wasn't hard to understand his need for some physical outlet. He was clearly a physically energetic man. She could imagine his playing sports, riding or racing, but it had never for one moment crossed her mind that he might actually enjoy getting his hands dirty!

So there was a rough and ready side to Sheikh Rashid al-Hazar that she had never for one moment suspected!

He was leading her along the pathway to a rear entrance of the palace, pausing on his way to deposit the tool-box in a work-room before striding up the wide stone steps to the main building. As Angela stepped ahead of him into the vestibule she immediately felt the welcome drop in temperature.

'Congratulations!' She turned to grin at him. 'You've done a good job. It's working perfectly!'

He nodded as he followed her into the vestibule and paused to pull the big door closed behind him. 'Yes, that's a big improvement,' he agreed, smiling. 'It was starting to feel like a steam bath in here.' Then his eyes twinkled mischievously. 'So, how are you going to thank me? Don't I deserve some kind of reward?'

As Angela met his eyes, her heart fluttered within her. He was standing very close to her, so close they were almost touching, and he was looking down at her through those thick black lashes with a totally unreadable look in his eyes.

He smiled slowly, making her blood leap. 'Well, *habibiti*,' he persisted. 'Don't you think I deserve a little thank you?'

Angela smiled lamely. 'Yes, I suppose so.' She could scarcely get the words out, her face felt so stiff with anxiety. If only she could think of some witty retort! But at that moment she was capable of only one single thought: was he or was he not going to kiss her?

She looked up into his eyes, endless pools of blackness, and felt suddenly quite giddy with the desire to get lost in them. To surrender to this hypnotic power he had over her. Blissfully to drown in the fierce dark passion of him.

Her lips parted involuntarily, waiting for the moment, for she knew she would not, *could* not resist him. She held her breath. Her eyelids fluttered. Every nerve-end in her body was alight with anticipation.

His hand was on her arm. He was bending towards her, fiery dark eyes burning into hers. And she felt herself almost die with pleasure as his lips came down to brush against hers. But they had barely made contact when she heard him murmur, 'What I'd like you to do for me is make us some coffee.'

Angela's eyes sprang open, her heart in an uproar, disappointment like ice-cold water flooding through her. For, though she was utterly appalled at herself, there could be no denying that, more than all the riches of Jahira, she had longed at that moment for Rashid's lips to consume her.

'Will you do me that favour?' His expression was oddly shuttered. 'While I go and change quickly, will you make us some coffee?'

'Of course. I'd be delighted.' She tried hard to smile, but her lips all at once felt frozen solid. She turned away awkwardly on legs made of rubber. Suddenly she could scarcely bear to look at him.

As he hurried upstairs, Angela headed for the kitchen where a couple of servants were busily working.

'No, I'll do it myself,' she pleaded, smiling stiffly, as each in turn tried to take over the coffee-making. '*Shokrun*. Thank you. I can manage perfectly.'

That was not quite true. Her hands were still shaking. But she desperately needed to busy herself with something in order to gather herself together.

She had make an utter fool of herself. She felt ashamed and humiliated. For she knew that he knew what had been going through her mind.

Despite her protests, as she made the coffee, a bubbling dark brew laced with aromatic cardamoms, a tray was prepared by one of the servants, complete with delicate, hand-embroidered tray-cloth and napkins, fragile Limoges china and tiny silver coffee spoons. And a generous-sized plate of assorted Arab cakes.

Angela was just setting down the silver coffeepot when Rashid walked into the room.

'All ready? That was quick.' He smiled at her approvingly. And again, to her chagrin, Angela's heart flared within her. But, in spite of his smile, there was now a distant air about him that seemed somehow to deny that anything had passed between them.

Angela felt her tension leave her. If he could pretend, then so could she. Meeting his eyes, she indicated the tray. 'Shall we go through to the sitting-room?' she asked him.

'I'll take the tray,' he intercepted quickly, as one of the servants stepped forward to do the honours. Then he was leading Angela out into the corridor, through the arches of the hallway to the sumptuous main sitting-room.

Angela watched him as he laid the tray on a long low table set between two deep-cushioned sofas. He had changed into a pair of cream-coloured trousers and a light blue shirt rolled back at the cuffs. And she could see that he had taken the time to quickly shower, for his brushed-back hair still glistened wetly.

'How do you like it? Black or white?' He glanced towards her as she sat on one of the sofas.

'Black. No sugar.' Angela was faintly astounded. She had assumed quite naturally that he would expect her to serve him.

He quickly poured and handed her her cup. 'Help yourself to a cake,' he told her. Then he poured for himself, spooned in some sugar, and lowered his tall frame into the sofa opposite her.

For a moment he drank in silence, then he regarded her over his coffee-cup. 'I'm glad to see that you've calmed down since our last meeting.' He laid down his cup. 'That was quite a little outburst.'

Angela cringed inwardly and avoided his eyes. She might have known he was bound to return to this subject. Suddenly she was wishing she hadn't agreed to join him for coffee.

When she did not answer—what could she say?—she could sense the amused smile on his face as he enquired, 'Are you in the habit of indulging in such violent emotional outbursts?' He paused for a moment. 'I had not suspected such strength of feeling in you.'

The observation brought a faint flush to Angela's cheeks. She had not suspected such strength of feeling in herself.

She raised her eyes to his and answered calmly, 'No, I'm not in the habit, as it happens. Only when someone really gets my back up.'

'And I got your back up?'

'It would appear so.'

'Indeed it would. How very strange...' He paused for a moment, black eyes on her. 'How very strange that I, of all people, should be capable of arousing such fierce emotions in you.'

'Oh, please don't think that!' Angela felt her blush deepen. 'It isn't *you* who arouses fierce emotions in me! It's the arrogant, unfeeling way you treat people!'

Rashid sat back and regarded her minutely. 'You are quite sure of that, are you, Angela?' he put to her.

'Of course I'm sure of it! *Absolutely* sure of it! As a man—I mean, as a person,' she quickly corrected herself, snatching her eyes away from his again, 'you have no effect on me whatsoever. But I object very strongly to the way you treat others.'

What she was saying was not quite true, and she suspected that he knew it. As a man he affected her deeply and powerfully, in a way that sent unquiet shivers through her soul. But it was perfectly true that she also disapproved of him. She clung on to that now for all she was worth, as, with a cool smile, he sat forward and leaned towards her.

'So, what did I do that day in my office that sent you into such a righteous rage?'

Angela cleared her throat. 'I don't know precisely. All I know is that you did something to upset Lalitha. I found her in the corridor, weeping her eyes out.'

He had the gall to smile and shrug. 'I wouldn't worry about that. Lalitha, like many other members of her sex, tends at times to over-react.'

'What do you mean by that?' What a chauvinistic remark! 'Don't you care that the poor girl was upset?'

Rashid shrugged again. 'I'm sure by now she's recovered. I don't really think there's any need for you to worry.'

'No, I don't suppose *you* would.' Angela's tone was cutting. 'I don't suppose you give a damn one way or the other.'

'Is that what you suppose?' His own tone had hardened. 'Considering you don't even know what happened, I must say you're very quick to make judgements.'

'Are you trying to tell me it was all Lalitha's fault? That she deserves to be treated the way you treat her?'

'And how do I treat her?'

'Like a servant.'

'Funny, I've never heard her complaining.'

'I don't suppose she'd dare complain! That's why you do it! You treat her like rubbish because she's too scared to stand up to you!'

He said nothing for a moment, but there was a dark look in his eyes, a look that warned her she'd gone quite far enough. He sat back abruptly against the cushions of the sofa. 'I suggest we drop this subject now. What happened between Lalitha and me is our private business. It really doesn't concern you in the slightest.'

So she had been put in her place, quietly but firmly. Angela said nothing as he picked up his coffee-cup, then raised it slowly to his lips and drank. As he laid it down again, he waved towards the cake plate. 'Help yourself to something,' he invited. 'The *konafa*, I find, are particularly delicious.'

Angela shook her head. 'No, thank you,' she answered. She, too, was a lover of these sticky Arab pastries, but she was not in the mood right now to oblige him.

Rashid helped himself and chewed slowly for a moment, dabbing the corners of his mouth with one of the crisp linen napkins. Then he sat back in his seat and surprised her by asking, 'How's your father? I hear he's improving.'

An alarm bell sounded in Angela's head. The enquiry, she knew, was not out of interest for her father.

She crossed her knees carefully and looked him straight in the face. 'He's improving greatly. By leaps and bounds. In fact, when I was at the hospital this morning, one of the nurses told me he could be released next week.'

'That is indeed good news.'

What a hypocrite he was! But she smiled sweetly. 'Yes, it is,' she agreed. 'Very good news. He won't be needing me around any more. He'll be able to stand on his own two feet.'

Rashid frowned a little. 'Do I misunderstand you—or are you suggesting that you might be planning to leave?'

What a display of innocence! The man deserved an Oscar! 'Not planning, exactly...' Angela regarded him meaningfully. 'More expecting that I might be required to leave.'

'For what reason?'

'For the very simple reason that I'm expecting my Residence Permit to be revoked.'

He remained poker-faced, his eyes unblinking. 'And why on earth should you be expecting that?'

Angela felt a flare of anger. Did he take her for a fool? Did he seriously think she had failed to understand the evil workings of his mind?

She leaned forward in her seat and told him frankly, 'I'm expecting it because I'm certain that that's your latest plan for me. Now that my father's on the mend, you can send me packing back to England with a clear conscience. Apart from anything else, I can't really see your forgiving me for the things I said to you the other day in your office. The ability to accept criticism isn't one of your strong points.'

He surveyed her for a moment, dark eyes revealing nothing. Then, to her surprise, he smiled. 'Perhaps that's because I'm not used to hearing any. Very few of the people I encounter feel free to speak to me as plainly as you do.'

'Because you're a sheikh?'

'The rank does have that effect.'

'You ought to be grateful.' Angela smiled with mild malice. 'You probably wouldn't like what you heard if people spoke their minds to you.'

To her further amazement, he responded by laughing. 'Yes, that thought has occurred to me, too,' he told her. 'Hypocrisy, in a cruel world, can have its merits.'

As he said it their eyes met, and the honesty in his, just for a moment, was naked and raw. There was not a trace of his usual arrogance, only the openly self-mocking candour of a man who was well aware of both his strengths and his weaknesses.

Angela tore her eyes away. The insight had unsettled her. Just for a moment she had felt that she might have misjudged him.

'You must have taken people's frankness badly when you were living in America.' She had been told that he had studied at the University of Chicago, and used that knowledge now to put some distance between them. Suddenly she had needed to reopen the gap between them. 'I'm sure nobody there cared that you were a sheikh.'

'I made sure that very few of them knew who I was. Only the University authorities and a couple of my tutors were aware of the fact that I was a sheikh.'

Frankly, that surprised her. Uneasily she persisted, 'Somehow, I can't see you mingling with the *hoipolloi*.'

'Can't you?' He smiled across at her. 'Well, you're very much mistaken. I enjoyed being one of the *hoipolloi*. For once I was just plain Rashid al-Hazar, treated exactly like anyone else, and it was a very welcome, very salutary experience. My years in the US were among the happiest of my life.'

'So, what happened to all these fine liberal attitudes? You obviously forgot to bring them back with you when it was time to come home.'

'What is appropriate in one particular part of the world may not be appropriate in another. One must learn to recognise what is appropriate to the circumstances and to be adaptable in these matters.' He paused for a moment, eyeing her closely. 'I believe that is something that even you are learning.'

'I? What do you mean?' She hadn't a clue what he was getting at.

'I mean, *habibiti*, that you have very pleasantly surprised me by displaying an appropriately sensitive touch in your handling of the women's page.'

'You mean you like it?' Her face lit up foolishly. 'You mean you actually approve of what I'm doing?'

He did not answer that directly. Instead, he told her, 'The readers like it.' He leaned back a little against the sofa, his hair very black against the bright red cushions. 'We've received several quite enthusiastic letters.'

'The new secretary told me.' Angela eyed him, wondering if he was also aware of the fact that there had been quite a few others of a more critical nature. She rather hoped that that had been kept from him.

Her hopes were instantly dashed. 'Naturally, we also have our critics, some fairly vociferous, I can tell you. But that is to be expected with anything new. As long as we continue on the lines that we're going along, I can see no reason why we shouldn't win them round eventually.'

Angela blinked at him. Had she misheard him? Was he actually associating himself with this hated project? Had she really heard him say 'we'?

As though in answer to her unspoken query, he added with a smile, 'We'll just have to wait and see.' Then he reached out and helped himself to another of the pastries, pushed the plate towards her and invited, 'Help yourself.'

This time Angela declined for a very different reason. Not out of anger at him but because she felt stunned. Either he was playing some elaborate game with her or else she had just witnessed a miraculous turnaround. But with someone as cagey as Rashid it was impossible to tell.

His eyes flitted over her as he chewed the sticky pastry. 'So what else have you been up to apart from hospital visiting and writing? Don't tell me it's been all work and no play?'

'Yes, I'm afraid it has.'

'What a pity.'

'I'm not complaining. It suits me quite well.'

He took another bite of the pastry and chewed on it slowly, his dark eyes thoughtfully studying her face. 'What about Vince, our dashing young photographer? Haven't you been seeing him?'

'Of course I've been seeing him.' For some reason the question irked her. 'I work with him, remember? I see him every day.'

'Outside work, I mean.' He was unruffled by her sharpness. 'I would have thought that, now that you're in a position to do so, you would have been taking the opportunity to entertain him.'

'And why should I do that?'

'You were most keen to do so earlier. What's the matter? Have the two of you fallen out?'

There was something most unsettling about the way he was quizzing her. His manner was at once intimate and somehow totally detached. And what right had he, anyway, to ask such personal questions?

She eyed him narrowly from across the coffee-table. 'Why on earth would I fall out with Vince? We get on very well. We're very good friends.'

'That's what I thought.' One black eyebrow lifted. 'So, if you're such good friends, why haven't you invited him round?'

'Perhaps I haven't needed to. Perhaps I've been visiting him at his place.' She hadn't, of course; she simply said it to rattle him. And she had the pleasure of seeing anger flare deep in his eyes.

'And have you?' he gritted, leaning suddenly towards her and laying the half-eaten pastry on his plate. 'That would not have been a very wise thing to do.'

'Even in the middle of the afternoon?' Suddenly she was enjoying leading him on.

'At any time of the day it would have been most unwise. A young woman who values her reputation does not go visiting a young man alone in his home.'

'Not even for an innocent cup of coffee and a chat? After all,' she added, stirring him up with gusto, 'that's what you and I are doing right now.'

'Except that we are not alone.' He spat the words at her like bullets. 'This house, as everyone knows, is full of servants. Vince, I happen to know, lives quite alone.'

There was something perversely pleasing about his anger. For once she had the feeling that she was in control. And, if she was honest, it was really rather flattering that he should feel so strongly about her having coffee with another man.

With deliberate bravado, she stretched out towards the cake-plate to help herself to a slice of *konafa*. 'What a fuss you're making.' She eyed him coolly. 'Nothing happened. You don't have to worry.'

But her hand never made contact with the pastry, for with whiplash speed he had reached out and grabbed her, his fingers fastening like a vice around her wrist.

There was a clatter as the sugar-bowl collided with the cream-jug, but his eyes didn't leave her face for a moment, as in a tone like rough sand-paper he commanded, 'Don't play games with me, *habibiti*! Did you or did you not visit Vince in his home?'

The speed and the ferocity of his reaction had shocked her. Angela felt her face pale and her eyes start from her head. 'Of course I didn't!' She tried to wrench her hand free. 'Now let me go! You're hurting me!'

His grip merely tightened. His eyes burned like hot cinders. 'Don't lie to me, *habibiti*! I want to know the truth!'

'It *is* the truth! Why would I go visiting Vince when I know it would only make people talk? Why would I take a risk like that when the two of us are only good friends?'

Rashid jerked her arm angrily, almost pulling her from the sofa. 'I don't give a damn what your re-lationship is with him! In fact I would understand perfectly if you were more than just friends. After all, he's an Englishman and you're an English girl. Nothing in the world could be more natural.'

He continued to glare at her, his eyes black and merciless. 'But if the two of you intend getting up to anything, I do insist that you be discreet about it. I will not have a member of my newspaper's staff being the subject of common gossip!' He jerked her arm again. 'Do I make myself clear?'

'Abundantly clear!' Pale-faced, Angela glared back at him, hating him with a fury she could barely control. Then, as he abruptly released her, she fell back against the cushions, her heart racing inside her like an express train.

At that moment, with a discreet cough, a servant entered the room and, speaking in Arabic, addressed himself to Rashid.

Rashid responded abruptly, then glanced briefly at Angela. 'You don't mind if I take a phone call in here, do you?'

She shook her head. 'Of course not,' she answered, as the servant silently crossed the room to hand Rashid a mobile phone.

Then she sank back against the cushions, still fighting to catch her breath, as Rashid launched into a conversation in Arabic. She felt shell-shocked and numb, her heart as tight as a drum within her. And it wasn't simply out of outrage at Rashid's behaviour. There was something far more lethal eating away at her.

For as her fury subsided to manageable proportions she realised with a sense of horror that it was the *cause* of his outburst rather than the actual outburst that had affected her.

She had believed for one brief misguided moment that he was angry with her because he was jealous. Lord knew where on earth the notion had sprung from, for it was about as far from the truth as it was possible to be. All he cared about was the good name of his newspaper. For her he cared less than the sand on his shoes.

And, though it should not have been so, to know that was crushing.

CHAPTER SEVEN

THE next week or so was a total upheaval. Quite out of the blue, Angela's father announced that he had decided to go back to England to convalesce.

'I've got a few months' leave due,' he told her one day at the hospital, 'and a lovely little cottage in the heart of Kent that I've been promising myself for years that I'll spend some time in.' He threw her a wink. 'I think now is the time. A few lazy months in the cool English climate are exactly what I need.'

His doctors had agreed with him wholeheartedly, and within forty-eight hours the arrangements had been made.

'You're sure you don't mind staying here on your own?' he enquired of Angela for the umpteenth time, as she drove him in her car to the airport. 'I'm sure MacLeish would let you go early if you asked him.'

'But I don't want to ask him. I'm enjoying my job.' With a reassuring smile, Angela squeezed her father's hand. 'I want to see the three months through and then I'll decide what I'm going to do.'

There was only one problem—which she hadn't mentioned to her father—and that was that, now that he was leaving Jahira, instead of moving back into the villa she would be obliged to go on staying at the palace. And she was finding that set-up daily more difficult, as every contact with Rashid seemed increasingly to undermine her. Suddenly her emotions were all over the place. She didn't like it and she didn't understand it.

Then something happened that only added to her confusion.

It was a couple of days after her father had left and Angela had nipped back to the palace for lunch. As was her custom, she headed for the kitchen, planning to fix something simple for herself, and was surprised to find a tall, dark-haired girl, dressed in a brightly coloured kaftan, piling chopped-up vegetables into a salad-bowl.

As Angela hesitated in the doorway, the girl came towards her, smiling broadly. 'Hi! You must be Angela! So, we meet at last! I'm Mariam, Rashid's sister.'

Angela shook the girl's hand in a state of shock and disbelief. Where was the cowed creature she had imagined, all dressed in black, huddled in her room? 'Pleased to meet you, too,' she answered, bewildered.

'I'm sorry I haven't been around much for the past few weeks. I've been terribly busy with some of my students.' Mariam returned to her salad-bowl and squeezed lemon juice into the contents. 'I'm making *tabbouleh*,' she grinned across at Angela. 'There's plenty for two. I hope you like it.'

Angela loved *tabbouleh*, the minty mixed salad that everyone seemed to consume in vast quantities in Jahira. She nodded. 'That's great.' Then, frowning, she enquired, 'What did you mean when you said you had students?'

Mariam tossed back her glossy black hair, tied in a band at the nape of her neck. 'The usual,' she explained, smiling. 'I'm a teacher.'

Angela blinked. 'You *work*?' she queried, biting back her real question: You mean Rashid lets you? Somehow she had the feeling that this bright intelligent girl would find such a question quite outrageous. She was very much her own person. That was obvious.

As it was, Mariam was smiling at her expression. 'Of course I work!' she laughed. 'And damned hard, I promise you! For the past few weeks I've been up to my ears helping some of my students cram for their exams. I've virtually been resident at the school!' She arranged some dishes of *mezze*— meat and vegetable starters—around the big bowl of salad in the centre of the table and invited Angela to join her.

'Come on, let's eat! And you can tell me all about yourself.'

It was the start of a warm and spontaneous friendship. Angela was amazed to discover how much they had in common. Together in the evenings, over dinner, they chatted about books and films and fashions, about England and Jahira and all the places they had visited. And Mariam, Angela discovered, was a well-travelled young woman, a frequent visitor to her parents who lived in Paris.

Sometimes, especially at the weekends, they were joined by Rashid.

'I hope you don't mind a man intruding,' he would tease them. 'I promise I won't bore you by talking about football and politics!'

In fact their little threesomes were far from boring. On the contrary, Angela enjoyed them thoroughly, even found herself looking forward to them increasingly. Since MacLeish had returned, she saw less of Rashid at the office, and in a strange way she missed that daily contact.

And it was good to be so at ease with him in his sister's company—for when he was around Mariam he shed all formality—and the warmth he so obviously felt for his sister at times seemed to reach out to include Angela, too.

It took a little getting used to. She was seeing an entirely new side to him. She was seeing a man who treated women with affection and respect.

Could this, too, she wondered, just be an act? She hated to admit it, but she found it unlikely.

Angela was working at her desk one afternoon when Sharma stopped by with a message. 'Sheikh Rashid wants to see you in his office right away.'

Instantly curious, Angela jumped to her feet. It wasn't often these days that she got a summons from the boss. But, just as she was gathering up her notepad and pencil, one of the phones on her desk began to ring.

Inevitably, it proved to be an urgent and complex phone call that ended up delaying her for a full five minutes. She hurried down the corridor to Rashid's office.

His door was ajar. Tapping lightly, she pushed it open apologetically. 'I'm sorry it took me so long to get here——' she began. But the words ground to a halt and she almost fell to the floor as her eyes took in the scene revealed before her: Rashid and Lalitha, standing in the middle of the office, in what appeared to be a fiery embrace!

The young Indian girl's arms were wrapped around his neck, his hands resting lightly on her waist. And both of them were laughing delightedly at one another, oblivious to the still, shocked figure in the doorway.

Totally pole-axed, Angela stood and stared at them. The last time she had set eyes on Lalitha she had been rushing from Rashid's office in a flood of tears. Whatever the problem between them that had evoked such emotion, it had evidently now been satisfactorily resolved.

Then Rashid caught sight of her. 'Come in,' he invited calmly, as, blushing furiously, Lalitha hurriedly disentwined her arms.

Angela obeyed. 'You wanted to see me?' Her voice sounded strange and flat to her own ears.

'Indeed I did.' Rashid was still smiling, apparently quite unable to conceal his good humour. Then, as Lalitha was about to head swiftly for the door, he reached out to catch her hand in his. 'I'll see you later.' He smiled and winked. 'I'm really glad you're back again.'

That scarcely needed saying, Angela found herself thinking, as with one of her elegant traditional bows—which, it suddenly struck Angela, was purely gracious, not grovelling—and still blushing furiously, Lalitha made her exit. And suddenly Angela was aware that her stomach was churning and that the room felt as though it were swimming round her head.

'Take a seat, please.'

She heard the words dimly and realised with a start that Rashid was talking to her. On rubber legs she crossed to the nearest chair and sank down on to it almost gratefully. She was aware that every inch of her body was trembling.

'I asked you here because I have something I want to discuss with you.' Rashid had seated himself behind his desk and was addressing her now in a totally composed fashion, as though nothing in the least untoward had happened.

Angela struggled to focus. 'Oh, yes?' she enquired politely, amazed that her voice sounded perfectly normal. Her tongue felt like a lump of blotting-paper in her mouth.

Now she understood what he had meant when he had said to her, 'What happened between Lalitha and me is our private business.' What he had meant was that they had had a lovers' quarrel.

Angela breathed in deeply. She had never suspected. And the revelation was like a dagger through her heart.

'These are what I want to talk to you about.' He was withdrawing from a drawer a sheaf of black and white photographs and laying them, fan-fashion, on his desk. 'I believe you're already familiar with them?'

Angela nodded. She had recognised them instantly. 'They're the pictures Vince took at that Bedouin encampment. Apparently, he just came upon it quite by accident.'

'So I understand. I think they're excellent. We must definitely find a way of using them.' He leaned across the desk towards her. 'I understand you're interested in doing a covering story?'

'Yes, I'd really like to.' Angela looked into his face, but somehow she couldn't quite meet his eyes. 'I know it's not strictly women's page stuff, but I could probably get something for the women's page out of it—and, anyway, I like doing the occasional general feature.'

As he nodded, she hurried on, 'MacLeish is agreeable. He said I should fix up for Vince to take me to the encampment. It's right out in the desert and I couldn't go myself—I'd probably end up getting lost.'

'So what are you waiting for? Have you spoken to Vince? We can't just sit on these photographs forever.'

At the sharpness of his tone Angela instantly reacted. How dared he? How dared he speak to her like that? First he had the nerve to subject her to the spectacle of that uncalled-for public embrace with his mistress—and now he had the arrogance to try and browbeat her!

Well, she would not have it! She looked him in the eye. 'I realise that.' Her tone was clipped. 'And, yes, of course I've spoken to Vince. The trouble is he's extremely busy. His assistant has just gone off on leave and he has the football tournament and the oil ministers' conference to cover all by himself. He simply hasn't got time to take me out there. That encampment isn't just at the end of the road, you know!'

Rashid raised one dark eyebrow, apparently surprised at her outburst. Then he sat back in his seat. 'How far is it?'

'I don't know exactly. A couple of hours' drive. The whole thing would take the best part of a day.'

He said nothing for a moment, then he leaned towards her. 'How's your diary? When's the next day you have free?'

Angela thought rapidly. 'I'm pretty busy, but I could juggle things around a bit to leave Wednesday free.'

'Then Wednesday it is.' He gathered up the photographs. 'Have your tape-recorder ready first thing on Wednesday morning.'

'But how...?' Angela blinked at him, not quite understanding. 'How am I supposed to get there?'

He raised dark eyes to her, their expression shuttered. 'Easy, *habibti*. I shall take you. You and I will spend a day together in the desert.'

Just twenty-four hours earlier the prospect would have thrilled her. Now Angela could think of no torture more cruel. For, now that she knew about his love-affair with Lalitha, just to look at him made her blood run cold. An entire day spent alone in his company was surely more than she could survive?

It had come as a shock when she'd faced up to her feelings. Over the past few weeks she'd had no idea just how important a role he'd come to play in her life.

Through sharing his home and the intimacies of his family life, she had come to regard him with a certain familiarity. She had grown to like him; she felt easy in his company; she had sensed some kind of bond developing between them.

And, much more dangerously, she realised belatedly, she had come to rely on this new closeness between them continuing. Perhaps even developing into something more special. Though she had never openly acknowledged it, that had been her dream.

It had been a foolish dream, rash and naïve, and now, without warning, it had been torn to shreds. At the thought bitter tears welled up in her eyes. Rashid already had a woman in his life. The place she had secretly longed for had already been filled.

In the office next day she found herself watching Lalitha, who, since her return, seemed like a woman reborn. A woman in love, Angela thought to herself bitterly, remembering the tenderness with which Rashid had told her, 'I'm really glad you're back again.'

She gritted her teeth. She must not torture herself. She must not think of Rashid and Lalitha together. In fact, she must not think of Rashid at all. Somehow she must conquer this dangerous infatuation.

On the appointed Wednesday he picked her up from the office in a huge white four-wheel-drive Toyota Land Cruiser.

'Sorry I'm a bit late,' he apologised quickly, as she climbed in and they set off for the city limits. 'I've been at my desk since six o'clock this morning, tying up loose ends to give me the day free. It took me a little longer than I'd expected.'

Angela flicked a glance at his composed dark profile, slightly shaded by the white *kaffiyeh*. 'You work too hard,' she told him lightly. 'It's not good for anyone to work the hours that you do.'

He turned to smile at her, making her heart squeeze. 'Is that a note of concern I detect in your voice?' He held her eyes. 'How very flattering.'

'Please don't be flattered.' She had turned away abruptly, hating herself for being so transparent. 'All I'm doing is repeating what Mariam's always saying. It's your sister, not I, who worries about you.'

She felt him shake his head. 'It's time Mariam was married. It's time she had a family of her own to worry about. Or perhaps——' he laughed softly '—perhaps it's time I was married. Then she could let my wife do the worrying for her!'

Angela swallowed hard and did not look at him. Suddenly her stomach was full of snakes.

Breathing slowly, she fished inside her bag, retrieved Vince's photographs and stared hard at them. 'I've brought the pictures,' she said, changing the subject, struggling to switch her brain into a safe professional groove, 'to help us identify who's who when we meet them.' She paused to flick through them, ignoring her trembling fingers. 'The women have such beautiful jewellery,' she added. 'I thought I might do a special little piece on that for the women's page.'

'Good idea.' Rashid nodded in approval. 'If you like, I can tell you something about the function of the jewellery—apart from the obvious decorative function. You can tell a lot about a Bedouin woman from the jewellery she wears.'

'What, for example?' Angela enquired automatically, grateful that they had moved to a less emotive topic. The thought of Rashid married had momentarily horrified her.

'Well, for a start, you can tell her position in society, whether she's rich or poor, married or single.'

Angela felt herself flinch and instantly stopped listening. There he went again, bringing up the subject of marriage. The snakes writhed and coiled as she snatched a quick glance at him. Could the reason for his sudden interest in the subject possibly be that he himself was contemplating matrimony?

A thought flared within her, making her body burn. Was that why Lalitha was looking so radiant? Had Rashid actually proposed marriage to her?

She cleared her throat. 'You can tell me all that later. I don't really need to know just yet.' Then she turned away deliberately to study the landscape, as they quickly left the outskirts of the city behind and started to head for the open desert.

Why should she care if he was marrying Lalitha? He meant nothing to her, she told herself fiercely. In fact, she should feel happy for the beautiful young secretary. It couldn't happen to a nicer girl.

They arrived at the encampment just before lunchtime, after a journey over endless undulating sand dunes that glistened beneath a sky of startling sapphire-blue.

First, a solitary palm tree came into view—and then rapidly turned into a cluster. 'We're here,' Rashid told her. 'This is it.' He nodded towards some roughly woven camel-hair tents pitched in the scanty patches of shade. 'Now let's see what kind of welcome we get.'

The welcome they received could not have been warmer. They were greeted by the head man, Abu Mahmoud, and instantly ushered into his tent.

On bare feet Angela stepped inside—her shoes, along with Rashid's and everyone else's, had been left in a neat row by the door—and, as she looked around her, her eyes grew wide. The tent was large, the size of a small room, and every inch of it was a blaze of colour, strewn with rugs and big soft cushions.

They were invited to sit, and sweet tea was brought as Rashid explained the purpose of their visit. And all the while Abu Mahmoud was nodding, stroking his grey beard and murmuring in Arabic.

At last Rashid turned to Angela. 'There's no problem,' he told her. 'You have permission to do your interviews. There's just one condition. Before you speak to anyone, you must agree to join Abu Mahmoud and his family for lunch.'

What followed was not so much lunch as a veritable feast. As the family gathered—grey-haired grandmas and bright-eyed children, so many it seemed the whole tribe must be related to Abu Mahmoud!—a whole roast sheep on a bed of rice was brought in on an enormous platter, with dishes of nuts, fresh dates and camel's milk, and jugs of precious water, fresh from the oasis.

It was mouthwateringly delicious. Angela ate till she was bursting. And, as she sat back against the cushions, she felt a warm glow of happiness and an unexpected sense of belonging.

She had scarcely understood a single word of the conversations that had been going on around her, yet never for one instant had she felt left out. By the use of sign language and with the occasional translation from Rashid she had managed to participate perfectly in the proceedings. And, besides, everyone was so friendly it was impossible to feel left out.

Nibbling on a fresh date, she glanced across at Rashid, seated opposite her, cross-legged, on the floor, laughing and chatting to the toothless old man beside him. It was hard to believe he was a prince of the realm, a powerful sheikh with a vast fortune to his name. Here he was being treated just like everyone else, and that, as he had once told her, was clearly the way he liked it.

She felt a surge of envy. Lucky Lalitha! But instantly she pushed the feeling away. Today was a special day. She would not spoil it by thinking thoughts that made her heart ache.

At last the coffee was brought, and Rashid leaned across to tell her, 'Abu Mahmoud says that, when you've had your coffee, you're free to start doing your interviews.'

'Tell him thank you and that it's been a wonderful meal. I've rarely felt so well-fed in my life!'

Their host appeared pleased as her message was translated. He grinned and nodded at her as Rashid informed her, 'He says it's been a pleasure and an honour for his family to play host to such a charming young lady.'

They spent the next couple of hours touring the small encampment, matching faces to the images on Vince's pictures and chatting to virtually everyone, it seemed to Angela. And for once Rashid let her take total charge.

'I'm just here to translate,' he told her, laughing. 'You decide who you want to speak to and what you want to ask.'

There was just one thing he insisted on. 'You tell me you've never ridden on a camel. Now's the time to put that right!'

They were standing in the little compound where the camels were tethered, with Ahmed, the young lad who looked after the beasts. Angela pulled a face. 'Do I really have to? I've never even ridden a horse before!'

Rashid took her arm. 'All the more reason. Come on. I want to see you sitting up there looking like the queen of the desert!'

Angela smiled, foolishly pleased by the way he had touched her. That old easiness between them, she sensed, was returning. But still, jokingly, she protested, 'Some queen of the desert! I'll probably end up falling flat on my face!'

As it turned out, she didn't—though she felt distinctly wobbly as the long-legged beast rose up from its knees, where it had crouched to allow her to climb into the saddle. Suddenly she understood why it was called the ship of the desert. It felt like being in a small rowing-boat in the middle of the high seas!

But, tucking her long skirt securely around her knees, she hung on tight to the leather pommel of the saddle, just as Rashid had advised her, and a moment later she had the glorious sensation of being perched among the palm trees, high above the tents.

'How does it feel?' Rashid was watching her, a relaxed and easy smile on his face.

'It feels great! I really like it!' She grinned from ear to ear. 'Ask Ahmed if he'll take me for a walk!'

With evident delight the young lad obliged, leading the camel and its increasingly confident rider round the perimeter of the compound.

'It takes a bit of getting used to,' she called down to Rashid, 'the way the camel sways from side to side. But I'm getting the hang of it. It's not so difficult.'

'I knew you'd manage it.' He was watching her with amusement. Then he narrowed his eyes at her and demanded, 'How would you feel about going for a real ride?'

'What do you mean, "a real ride"?' She glanced down at him curiously.

'I mean a gallop across the desert.' He came to stand beneath her, eyes bright, as he looked up at her. 'I'll be with you. Are you game?' he challenged.

Angela paused for just a moment, feeling a thrill of expectation as she looked down into his upturned face. 'Of course I'm game.' She held his gaze for a moment. Suddenly her heart was racing in her chest.

'OK, you're on!' Rashid turned to Ahmed and invited the young lad to give him a leg-up. Then with one athletic bound he was seated behind Angela and reaching down to take the reins in his hands.

As they moved out of the compound, watched by an approving throng of onlookers, Angela was feeling light-headed with excitement. Partly at the prospect of the ride before her—her fingers were curled tightly around the pommel of the saddle—but to a far greater extent by the simple fact of having Rashid so physically near.

His torso was curved forward as he guided the camel, his chest and shoulders pressed hard against her back, the insides of his thighs squeezed firmly against her flanks, his strong arms seeming almost to embrace her. And from time to time, as his chin brushed her ear, she caught a tantalising waft of the clean masculine scent of him.

And the strangest sensations were burning within her. Her flesh suddenly ached with a fierce sweet yearning.

Without her realising it, their mount had speeded up to a canter as they headed out into the open desert.

'Are you all right?' Rashid's murmur against her ear brought her instantly out of her dream.

She nodded. 'I'm fine.'

'Shall we go a little faster?' His arm slid round her waist, drawing her more securely, more intimately against him.

Angela suppressed a shudder of excitement and sheer pleasure. 'Anything you say,' she answered with abandon.

She felt his grip tighten a little as he curved more firmly against her, then with a snap of the reins the camel lurched forward and suddenly they were racing like the wind across the desert, Rashid's head-dress flying, Angela's hair whipping out behind her, a cloud of golden sand billowing in their wake.

'Are you enjoying it, *habibiti*?' His lips brushed her ear.

'It's marvellous! I love it!' She gasped for breath, one hand clutching at the pommel of the saddle, the other hanging on hard to Rashid's forearm.

'Don't stop!' she implored him. 'I could go on forever!'

She felt him laugh against her cheek and, suddenly reckless, she longed to turn round and gaze into his face. She half turned, awkwardly, her heart twisting with emotion, and felt a shock of unexpected pleasure as her eyes instantly met the velvet dark gaze.

He smiled at her strangely. *'Habibiti,'* he murmured. Then, just as she was about to turn away again, he leaned towards her and, to her astonishment, kissed her.

Delight, like fingers caressing the keys of a piano, went rippling deliciously up and down her spine. Her stomach squeezed into a knot and suddenly her heart was beating like a drum. Breathlessly, she turned back to face the front again, though her eyes could no longer see where she was going. All at once she was alight with a sense of exhilaration. All at once her heart was flying on a magic carpet.

'Shall we go back now? They'll be wondering where we are.' Rashid was wheeling the camel round in a wide shimmering arc.

Angela nodded reluctantly. 'OK,' she murmured. The last thing she wanted was to return to normality.

But all too soon they were slowing down, as they came once more in sight of the encampment. Then they were heading for the compound and Ahmed was taking the reins as a group of delighted on-lookers burst into spontaneous applause. Rashid slid to the ground as Ahmed bade the camel kneel to allow Angela to dismount from the saddle.

'*Shokrun.*' She thanked him; then, on faintly shaky legs, she followed Rashid out of the compound.

It was time to leave then. As his family gathered round them, they thanked Abu Mahmoud for his kind hospitality. The old man took Angela's hand in his and said something to her in Arabic.

Rashid smiled as he translated. 'He says to tell you you're welcome to come back any time.'

Angela blushed with pleasure. 'Tell him thank you—and that I hope one day to take up his offer.'

Then they were climbing into the Toyota Land Cruiser and setting off beyond the palm trees to the empty desert, Angela aware of a sharp tug of regret inside her. In spite of what she'd said, she knew she was unlikely ever to see these people again. They had been no more than a bright brief interlude in her life.

Like Rashid, she thought wistfully, casting a secret glance at him. And for a moment she was totally overcome by the rush of pain that welled up inside her. Their lives were set on such different paths. She had no place in his, nor he in hers, in spite of the wonderful renewal of closeness that she had felt with him today.

She breathed in deeply. Why must she torture herself? Why not just accept the way things were and stop hankering after what could never be hers?

As she closed her eyes, her thoughts flew to that kiss. But it had meant nothing, she chided herself, nothing at all. It had been a light-hearted gesture, simple and spontaneous, reflecting the excitement of the moment and the good humour of the day.

She pushed the memory away and opened her eyes again—and all at once become aware that they were literally hurtling along!

'What's the hurry?' She glanced across at Rashid. 'Why on earth are you driving so fast?'

He frowned and kept his eyes fixed straight ahead. 'I'm afraid it all took rather longer than I'd intended. I'd hoped to get back on to the main road before it grew dark, but it looks as though we're not going to make it.'

Angela glanced at her watch. He was absolutely right. It was almost five o'clock, only a few minutes to sunset. She felt a flurry of worry. They were miles from anywhere. 'What are we going to do?' she asked him.

To her amazement, in reply, he drew the car to a halt, pulled on the handbrake and turned round to look at her. 'What I suggest we do is make a virtue of necessity. Since there's no way we can make it to the main road in time, let's take advantage of being stuck out here amid the sand dunes.'

Angela blinked at him. What on earth was he suggesting? As he spoke, he had laid one arm along the back of her seat. 'Take advantage of being stuck out here—how?' she enquired uncertainly.

He threw her a wink. 'We're not in any hurry. We've nothing to lose—except half an hour or so of our time.'

'I don't know...' Suddenly Angela's heart was fluttering. Surely he couldn't be suggesting what she was thinking he was suggesting?

But maybe he was. 'Let's get out of the car. It's too cramped; we'll be more comfortable outside.' Then, before Angela could utter another sound, he had pushed open the driver's door and jumped down on to the sand. An instant later, her own door was opened. He held out his hand to help her down.

Angela hesitated. Her heart was thumping inside her. 'I don't understand... Where are we going? Why are we getting out of the car?'

Rashid reached for her with one hand and pointed with the other. 'We're going to climb to the top of that sand dune over there.'

'Whatever for?' Still she was uncertain. They were in the middle of nowhere. She was totally at his mercy. And who knew what he had in mind?

Then, with the lift of one eyebrow, he enlightened her. 'You and I are going to watch the sunset, *habibiti*.'

CHAPTER EIGHT

ANGELA stumbled from the Land Cruiser, feeling faintly foolish.

'Have you ever watched the sun set in the desert?' Rashid asked her as, taking her by the hand, he led her across the sand.

'No, never.' She shook her head as she hurried to keep up with him.

'Then I can promise you a sight to remember. There is nothing more beautiful than a desert sunset.'

They were clambering up the side of the sand dune now, the warm sand slipping beneath their feet. 'Take off your shoes,' Rashid instructed, pausing to remove his own, along with his socks, and toss them down the side of the dune. 'The climb is easier in bare feet.'

Feeling like a small child on an outing, Angela obeyed, slipping off her strappy sandals and flinging them with gay abandon to the bottom of the sand dune.

Then Rashid was grabbing her by the hand again. 'I'll race you to the top!' And, laughing and tripping and falling all over one another, they were scrambling like two schoolchildren towards the summit.

Breathless with laughter, they collapsed at the top, Rashid ripping off his head-dress and tossing it aside. 'It's years since I've done this,' he told her, smiling. 'When I was a kid we used to come out to the desert a lot. We used to climb sand dunes the way English kids climb hills.'

Angela looked across at him, her heart turning over strangely. She had never been able to imagine him as a young boy before, but now, quite easily, she could.

And suddenly another thought occurred to her. She leaned towards him. 'I want to apologise for something I said to you a long time ago.'

Rashid patted the sand beside him. 'Come and sit here next to me. I'm all ears,' he invited, smiling.

She obeyed with pleasure, leaning lightly against him as he slid one arm around her shoulder. 'I once accused you of being showy. I accused you of believing that big was beautiful.' She looked up into his face. 'Do you remember?'

'Of course I remember. We were in my office.' His hand stroked her arm. 'So, what about it?'

Angela shrugged. 'I think I misjudged you. Now that I've been out in the desert and seen its hugeness and its endless emptiness, I think I can understand why you need plenty of space around you. It must be pretty claustrophobic being stuck in an office block when for generations you've been used to living in the open desert.'

Rashid laughed. 'That's what my grandfather used to say. He was the last of our family to live as a true Bedouin.' Then he turned to look at her.

'You know something, *habibiti*? I think you're starting to understand this country of mine a little.'

As he spoke his fingers continued to caress her bare arm, so naturally Angela wondered whether he was aware that he was doing it. And it was the total naturalness that made the gesture so pleasing, as though they were old intimate friends, totally at ease with one another.

Then, as she leaned happily against him, he pointed towards the west. 'It won't be long now. Keep your eyes on it.'

Angela raised her eyes to the fiery red ball that seemed to hover over the horizon. 'It looks so huge,' she murmured, wide-eyed. 'I've never seen a sun—or a moon, come to that—as huge as they seem to be in Jahira.'

'That's because we're so near the equator.' His breath was in her hair, sending shivers across her scalp. 'That's also why the sunsets here are so rapid, why there's virtually no dusk to speak of. In less than half an hour it'll be completely dark.'

'Oh, look, it's sinking! It's touching the horizon!' Angela felt a thrill of excitement as the moment finally came. She had seen many sunsets in her life, but, as Rashid had promised, this one was truly special.

'I wonder where it goes to?' he teased, fingers stroking her. 'It looks as though it's melting into the sand.'

'Maybe it is,' Angela teased back. 'Maybe out there in the middle of the desert there's a big orange pool of liquid sun.'

'What a lovely thought.' He turned to look at her. 'Do you think we ought to try and find it?'

Angela shook her head, her heart squeezing within her, and glanced away towards the dying sun. 'We would only be disappointed if we failed.'

He laughed against her hair. 'You're far too cautious. Think how wonderful it would be if we succeeded.'

All that was left now of the big fiery ball was a dark red smudge against the horizon. 'That's it. It's all over,' Rashid murmured, a note of almost wistful regret in his voice. Then, as he paused and shifted his position in the sand, Angela fully expected that he was about to stand up. She herself was half tensed to do likewise when, to her surprise, he turned round to face her, the hand on her shoulder slipping to the back of her neck.

'I'll bet you wouldn't have seen that if you'd come with Vince.' He smiled lopsidedly in the moonlit darkness. 'Maybe, after all, it was worth putting up with me in his place.'

As Angela looked back at him something stirred within her, a sudden anxious need to set the record straight. 'Really, you're wrong about Vince and me. There's nothing between us. We're friends and workmates, but that's absolutely all.'

The fingers on her neck slid up into her hair. He seemed to lean towards her. 'Convince me,' he challenged.

'How can I convince you?' Her scalp was in flames.

He leaned a little closer. 'Try,' he persuaded.

All she could see were his eyes, which devoured her. As black as the night and full of the night's mysteries. 'Vince has a girlfriend in England,' she muttered, well aware that this was not the manner of convincing he had intended. 'They're going to be married as soon as he's saved enough money. He's very much in love with her. He's not interested in me.'

'I'm still not convinced.' Rashid's voice was low and husky. Suddenly his free hand was tilting her face, and she could feel his breath, sweet and warm, against her skin.

Angela swallowed, feeling her heart burst inside her. 'And, what's more,' she elaborated, 'I'm not interested in him.'

He bent to touch her lips then, briefly, tantalisingly, making her blood leap in her veins. 'You're sure of that?'

'Quite sure.' She was dying. Her whole body was shrieking with the agony of wanting him.

'And who are you interested in?' Once more he brushed her lips. His eyes burned into her, making her tremble.

'No one,' she spluttered. 'There's no one in my life.'

'So if I kiss you, you will not be thinking of another?'

Angela shook her head wordlessly. 'Oh, no,' she promised him. But what about you? What about Lalitha? She longed to ask the question, yet she feared to hear his answer. She closed her eyes. 'No, no,' she said again.

'In that case...' He brushed her lips again, drawing her against him. She could feel his heart beating. She could smell the clean smell of him. 'In that case...' he began again. But, once more, he did not finish. As his lips pressed against hers, there was no more need for words.

They fell against the sand, arms twining round each other, lips locked in a deep, fierce, endless kiss, his hand in her hair, hers tugging through his, their bodies pressed hungrily against one another.

Angela gasped for breath. She could not believe it, the raw uninhibited way he made her feel. Suddenly her senses were a dazzle of bright colours, sparks flying from her skin wherever he touched her, a thunder of emotion clamouring in her brain.

His lips were an instrument of irresistible torture, driving her crazy with wicked plundering kisses. Caressing, teasing, torturing and devouring her, awakening deep inside her a warm throb of desire.

'Habibiti, habibiti...' He scattered kisses over her face, igniting her skin with every touch of his lips. And, as his lips blazed a trail across her face and her neck, his hands proceeded to explore her aching body.

As soft as gossamer, his hands caressed her, sweeping down the length of her arms. And, as he pushed back the elbow-length sleeve of her blouse to mould her shoulder with his hand, one finger trailed softly along her naked collarbone, sending a dart of excitement driving through her.

Her breasts ached for his touch. She pressed against him, her nipples hard and erect beneath the cotton of her blouse.

But he was taking his time about pleasuring her senses. As her own fingers tightened urgently in his hair, clutching at the thick black silkiness of it, he resumed his unhurried exploration, his hands leaving her shoulders to skim the dip of her waist, then with loving appreciation to mould the curve of her hips.

They were lying on their sides, he half leaning over her, and, as his hands moved round from her thighs to her buttocks, in one firm movement he drew her savagely against him so that she could feel, as hard as a boulder, the evidence of his arousal against her stomach. A spasm of animal passion went knifing through her.

With a gasp deep in her throat her hands fluttered to his shoulders, then slid down to press hard against his lower back, as though to join his body to her own through the strictures of their clothing.

He took her by surprise then as one hand swept up to capture one eager, swollen breast.

Angela was aware of a dizzy sensation as for one moment, almost brutally, he moulded the sensitive flesh. Then she had to bite her lip not to cry out loud as, in one smooth movement, he undid her blouse and impatiently pushed aside her bra to allow his hand access to her warm tingling flesh.

Dexterously he held both breasts in one hand, the heel of his hand lightly grazing one nipple while his fingers mercilessly squeezed and teased the other.

As her back arched in pleasure, he rasped against her ear, 'Shall I drive you crazy, *habibiti*? Shall I make you lose your mind?' Then, when she could manage no more than a groan in response, he growled a warming. 'You'd better be careful. This is going to drive me crazy, too.'

In one movement he had rolled her over on to her back, so that he was lying on top of her, looking down at her. His eyes flared with a passion that made her blood leap and it crossed Angela's mind, in a hazy kind of fashion, that perhaps he had reached the point of no return. Perhaps right here in the middle of the desert, beneath a night sky filled with stars, she was about to be divested at last of her virginity. The thought only served to excite her even more.

Both hands were on her breasts now, teasing, torturing. He bent to kiss her face. 'Are you crazy yet? Shall I make you crazier, *habibiti*?' Then, before she could respond, his lips were moving lower to close hungrily, greedily, over one blood-gorged nipple.

He had not lied to her. He was indeed driving her crazy as he pulled on her swollen, sensitised flesh, sharp teeth sending wrenches of fiery longing through her, his tongue hot as it strummed without mercy.

'More? Shall I give you more?' As she gasped for breath, her senses reeling beneath the on-slaught, she was aware that her skirt had ridden up around her waist, exposing her golden thighs and stomach. His weight shifted a little, exposing her near-nakedness, then she shuddered as his hand swept down between her thighs and, for one tantalising moment, lingered there.

And she was aware of one sensation only. That with every fibre of her being she desired him.

But, once again, he was destined to surprise her. His next move, she had expected, would be to remove her lacy briefs, but instead he pulled her skirt down over her thighs and looked down at her with cloudy dark eyes.

'At this moment I want nothing more in the world than to make love to you.' His voice was gruff. 'But, alas, it cannot be.'

With a harsh sigh he rolled away from her to lie on his back and stare up into the star-filled sky.

'Why?' She had to ask him, though it sounded shameless. She felt shocked, as though she had been dropped down from the stars.

He reached for her hand and raised it to his lips, but still he kept his eyes averted. 'It would not be right. It is not meant to happen. You and I ...' He let his voice trail away on a sigh. 'We do not belong,' he added finally.

Angela dared not look at him. Her heart was in turmoil. He was thinking of Lalitha, the girl he was to marry.

And she was suddenly filled with the bitter bile of shame as in a soft compassionate voice she heard him tell her, 'You would have regretted it. Believe me, I know. You are not the type to have sex without love.' He squeezed her hand softly. 'You know I am right.'

Angela turned her head away. She felt sick inside. How could she have allowed herself to be carried away like that when she knew he was involved with another woman?

As he squeezed her hand again, she turned to look at him. And in that instant, as she looked into his face, she knew the answer to her question.

He did not love her, but the worst had happened. She had fallen in love with him.

The certain knowledge that it was so sat like a dead weight in Angela's heart. She had believed she was in the grip of a mere infatuation. Something she could fight against and conquer. But the truth was much simpler and far more terrifying. How did one escape from the stranglehold of love?

She asked herself that question all the way back to Jahira City, but as they drew up outside the palace she was still without an answer.

Rashid turned to her as she started to climb from the car. 'I hope you're not upset about what happened back there? You've been very quiet. You've scarcely said a word.'

Angela tried to smile. 'Neither have you.' Though the reason for his silence, she was perfectly well aware, had been the need to give his full attention to his driving. Driving at night along unlit desert roads was a task that demanded total concentration. She added quickly, 'Of course I'm fine. Why on earth should I be upset?'

'I just wondered.' To her horror, he touched her hand. She didn't want him to touch her. She wanted to flee. 'What happened back there...' He smiled strangely. 'I guess we just both got a bit carried away. But it didn't mean anything.' He frowned apologetically. 'I certainly didn't mean any disrespect.'

'Of course not. Of course not. No need to apologise. As you said, we both just rather lost our heads.'

'That's OK, then.' Rashid nodded. 'We can just forget it ever happened.' Then he released her hand and pushed open his door. 'Let's go and get cleaned up. I could do with a shower.'

For her part, once she was upstairs in her room, Angela took refuge in a long, hot bath. She sank into the bubbles and closed her eyes and tried to shut out the pain that gripped her heart. But the words he had spoken echoed endlessly inside her.

'It didn't mean anything... forget it ever happened.'

If only he knew that it had meant the whole world to her. That she would never forget as long as she lived.

Tears streamed miserably down her cheeks to mingle with the soapy, scented water. And not only would she remember, she would treasure the memory—with only one regret. That he had not made love to her completely.

For, by denying her that ultimate physical intimacy, he had denied her the wonder of belonging to him, even briefly.

She grabbed for the soap and with sudden energy began rubbing down her arms and shoulders. Fool! she chastised herself. Fool to love him! You knew from the start that you could never have him! Even if there had been no Lalitha, our lives are too different. *We do not belong.*

Struggling for control, she tried to laugh at herself. What an idiot she was! What an utter clown!

But laughter wouldn't come. It died in her throat, as she sank into the bubbles and covered her face with her hands.

It would be impossible now for Angela to stay on in Jahira. Every day around Rashid was like a stake through her heart.

Not that she could have accused him of pressing his company on her. On the contrary, these days he seemed as anxious as she was to keep their encounters to a minimum. They saw each other seldom, but even seldom was too often. Just a glimpse of his face could tear her heart to pieces.

And Lalitha, too. Seeing Lalitha was painful. There had been no announcement of an impending marriage, but Lalitha had that unmistakable air about her of one who was hugging a secret to her bosom. Sooner or later, the announcement must come.

So, Angela had no doubts about what she had to do. At the first opportunity she spoke to MacLeish and informed him of the decision she'd had no choice but to come to.

His face fell with disappointment. 'I thought you liked the job. I was sure you'd opt to stay on once the three months were up.'

Angela bit her lip and dropped her eyes away. 'I do enjoy the job,' she assured him, feeling awkward. In other circumstances, if only he knew, she would have loved to have stayed on. 'But I feel it's time I got back to England. I've been away for long enough.'

'Are you worried about your father?' MacLeish was reluctant to accept her decision. 'I don't think you need be. He seems to be doing fine. The last time I spoke to him he sounded terrific.'

'No, it's not because of my father...' Angela floundered for a moment. The excuses she was offering sounded feeble, but there was no way she could tell MacLeish the truth. She took a deep breath. 'Look, I'm sorry to disappoint you. Truly I am. You gave me a wonderful opportunity and for that I'm really grateful. But we did agree...' She looked across at him appealingly. 'We did agree that after three months either of us could terminate the arrangement.'

MacLeish sensed her discomfort. 'Of course, lass, you're right. You have every right to leave if you want to.' He sat back in his chair and smiled kindly across at her. 'It's just that I'll be sorry to lose you. You've made an invaluable contribution to the paper.'

Angela thanked him sincerely. His praise meant a lot to her. Then she started to stand up as his phone began to ring.

But, before she could make her exit, MacLeish adjured her, 'I think it would be a good idea if you went and had a word with Sheikh Rashid. I'm sure he would appreciate being told in person. And you'd better do it tonight. He's off to Australia tomorrow morning. He may not be back before you leave.'

Angela felt her heart shrivel inside her. Since their day together out in the desert she had exchanged no more than a few brief words with Rashid, and she had prayed that she might be allowed to leave without having to confront him.

Yet now, as MacLeish reached to pick up his phone, she found herself agreeing, though it made her heart sick. 'OK,' she mumbled. Then she staggered out of the door. How on earth could she bring herself to do it?

Yet she had to do it, now, right this minute, for, if she waited, her nerve would surely fail her. On stiff legs, with a stiff smile pinned to her face, she forced herself to continue down the corridor till she came to the door marked 'Managing Director'.

Taking a deep breath, she tapped. Perhaps the gods would be merciful. Perhaps, by some miracle, he had already gone home.

There was a brief pause, during which she almost dared to hope. Then a wrenchingly familiar voice bade her, 'Come in!'

Like a robot, Angela stepped into the room, scarcely daring to focus on the figure behind the desk. She walked halfway across the carpet and came to a stop. 'I've come to see you,' she told him in a strange voice.

He had been bent over his desk, leafing through some papers. He glanced up now and, with a light smile, told her, 'Yes, I can see that.'

The smile, his easy manner, the familiar tone of voice tore at Angela's heart like red-hot pincers. Suddenly, it was almost too painful to breathe.

As she stood there, galvanised, he waved towards a chair. 'Why don't you take a seat? Make yourself comfortable.'

She could not do that. The seat was much too close to him. She would feel trapped if she were to sit so near.

She clenched her fists at her sides. 'There's no need. Really. What I have to say won't take a moment.'

As he frowned a little and sat back in his chair, Angela could sense that he had picked up her nervousness. 'What is it, Angela?' he enquired, watching her.

His use of her name caused her anxiety to double. She had to force the words from her lips, like squeezing a rope through the eye of a needle. 'I've come to tell you I'm leaving,' she informed him.

Even to her own ears, the statement sounded harsh. She had not meant to put it quite so bluntly. It had been her intention to soften it with some kind of lead-in.

'I see.' He seemed to grow very still for a moment. Then he sat back in his chair. 'And when are you leaving?'

'As soon as possible. As soon as I can tie up all my loose ends. Within the next ten days or so, I expect.'

'Very interesting.' The black eyes were on her. 'And am I one of your "loose ends", as you call them? Is that why you have taken the trouble to come here to see me?'

A shaft of helpless hurt went driving through her. If only that really was all he meant to her—an untidy loose end that required tying up.

She told him frankly, 'It was MacLeish who told me to come to see you. Otherwise, I would not have bothered you.'

'I expect you wouldn't.' His tone was crushing. 'No doubt you would have crept off without a word. No doubt you wouldn't even have taken the trouble to say goodbye to me.'

It was quite true, she wouldn't. But not out of rudeness. Not for the reasons that he seemed to think!

She started to protest, then dropped her gaze away. How could he even begin to understand when there was no way she could open up her heart to him?

'So, why are you leaving?' His eyes were still on her. 'And why so suddenly? Is there any special reason?'

Angela cleared her throat. 'The reason is very simple. My three-month trial is up next week and I think it's time for me to go back to England.'

'I see. You're tired of novelty.' His tone was cutting. 'And there's nothing else here worth staying on for.'

She threw him a hard look. 'That's right,' she answered. 'My adventure is over. It's time to go home.'

'Good for you.' His tone was barbed wire. 'It must be nice to have no conscience.'

'Conscience?' she frowned at him.

'Yes, conscience!' he thundered. 'No conscience and not a gram of responsibility. Quite evidently you don't give a damn about the mess you're leaving behind you!'

'What mess?'

'The women's page. The one you fought so hard for. Who the hell's going to run that when you're gone? You started something and now you're walking out on it! You're really terrific! You couldn't care less!'

'I do care! Of course I care!' The accusation stung her. 'I put my heart and soul into that women's page! How can you say a thing like that?'

'I can say it because it's true!' His eyes were merciless. 'You couldn't care less about the women's page! Or the *News*! Or Jahira! If you ask me, you don't give a damn about anything but yourself!' Suddenly his fist thumped down on his desk, causing the very walls of the office to tremble. 'Go on, get back to England! What are you waiting for? Get out of here!'

Angela was tempted to turn around and storm out of the office, pausing only to slam the door behind her. How dared he accuse her in such a fashion? But she straightened her shoulders and proceeded to defend herself.

'I have no intention of leaving the women's page in a mess. It so happens I have so much material in hand that it'll quite happily run itself for several weeks—and MacLeish is prepared to handle it personally until he can find a suitable new editor.'

'How very convenient for your conscience!' His tone was openly contemptuous. 'I believe you've actually talked yourself into believing that your totally irresponsible and unprofessional behaviour is in fact perfectly laudable.'

Angela thrust her chin at him, anger flaring. 'There's nothing unprofessional about what I'm doing! MacLeish and I had an agreement. I'm perfectly entitled to be leaving now.'

'Entitled, entitled!' He bit the words at her, dismissing her argument with a wave of his hand. 'Spare me your pathetic rationalisations and just get of of here. I'm a busy man.'

'Don't worry, I'm going!' Angela glared at him. 'I have no desire to listen to any more of your ravings!'

She turned swiftly on her heel, her heart pounding inside her. But for some reason at the door she paused and turned round to face him.

The black eyes narrowed. 'Well?' he demanded. 'What are you waiting for? Have you something more to say?'

Angela shook her head.

'Then what are you waiting for?'

As she looked into his face she felt the life leave her body. This was the very last time she would ever see him, and the only emotion she could see in his eyes was hate.

She took a deep breath. 'Nothing,' she whispered.

Then she turned around stiffly and reached for the door-handle. And, with her heart turned to ashes, she strode out through the door.

CHAPTER NINE

AFTER that, the days passed with frightening speed. In no time at all it was time for her to leave.

Angela packed her bags with a heavy heart. It was just over three months since she had arrived in Jahira, but those three tumultuous months had changed her forever—turned her inside-out and burned a brand on her soul. Yet, though her heart was raw and bleeding inside her to know she would never see Rashid again, she would not have denied herself the experience of having loved him. Her love had been doomed even before it had been awakened, but she would treasure it until the day she died.

There was only one tragedy, about which she could do nothing, one shadow she would never erase from her life. For she knew with total certainty that never again would she love any man as she had loved Rashid. Even if she lived for a thousand years, no man would ever move her again as he had. And to know that was to recognise an endless emptiness in her soul.

Mariam and MacLeish came to see her off at the airport.

'I'll miss you, Angela,' Rashid's sister hugged her warmly, and even MacLeish looked slightly emotional as he told her,

'Look after yourself, lass, and good luck in your career. I just know you have a wonderful future ahead of you.'

Angela smiled back at them, scarcely able to speak. 'Thanks for everything. I'll never forget either of you.'

Then she was being ushered through Passport Control and turning one final time to wave farewell before being swallowed up in the crowd.

And that was it. As though in a dream, twenty minutes later Angela boarded the plane. Then she was buckling her seatbelt and preparing for take-off, scarcely even aware of what she was doing. All she could think of were MacLeish's parting words: 'I just know you have a wonderful future ahead of you.'

He had meant them kindly, but they had turned her heart to stone.

For, until he had spoken them, it was as though she had believed that her world would end the moment she was airborne. Like the final fade-out of some movie she had envisaged the plane heading for the horizon, then in one bright flicker being swallowed up into some merciful void where no future existed.

Instead, all too harshly, MacLeish's words had reminded her that what awaited her was an endless and unbearable future. A future in which she must go on living and striving when she no longer had anything to go on living for.

For in that future there would be no Rashid, except as a constant pain in her heart.

Suddenly she could not breathe. Her soul filled with tears. She gazed emptily into space. 'How shall I survive?'

'Just a quick drink, Angela. You could catch the next train.'

'I can't. I promised my father I'd be on the early one.' Angela smiled apologetically into disappointed blue eyes. 'Perhaps we can have a drink together some time next week?'

'That's what you always say.' Tim smiled good-naturedly. 'You're an extremely difficult lady to pin down.'

Angela glanced away. She had been told that a lot recently. 'I don't mean to be,' she offered apologetically. 'It's just that . . .'

But Tim saved her the trouble of having to search for some explanation. 'Off you go, or you really will miss that train of yours!' He smiled at her kindly. 'Have a good weekend. I'll see you on Monday.'

Angela threw him a grateful smile. 'You have a good weekend, too.' Then, with her weekend-bag slung over her shoulder, she dived down the steps of Blackfriars underground station. She had fifteen minutes to get to Victoria main-line station to catch the seventeen-fifty commuter train to Sittingbourne in Kent.

A breathless thirteen minutes later she had miraculously made it and, even more miraculously, had managed to find herself a seat. Then, right on time, they were drawing away from the platform and heading off on the journey south.

Angela gazed out of the window, feeling guilty. Though she made a point of phoning him regularly, just to make sure that he was OK, it was over a month since she had last seen her father. And she felt deeply ashamed of the way she had been neglecting him, in spite of the fact that he never complained.

'Don't worry about me,' he always told her when they spoke and she invariably promised to visit him soon. 'I'm doing just great down here on my own. And I'm sure you've got far better things to do than keep coming down to visit your old dad.'

Angela smiled wryly to herself. If only he knew! He probably imagined that her life up in London was one long endless round of socialising. Parties, theatres, exciting dinner dates. And she, coward that she was, just let him believe it. It was easier that way. It saved the need for explanations.

She sighed as the train rolled through the suburbs of London. Her father, with his new-found interest in golf and fishing, probably had a far busier social life than she did. Which would not, she reminded herself, be a difficult achievement. She virtually had no social life at all.

Sure, she saw old girlfriends from time to time, and she had no shortage of invitations from new colleagues like Tim. But, these days, her heart just didn't seem to be in anything. Nothing was any fun any more.

And it was a hopeless way to continue. She realised that. She must snap herself out of it. She must start living again.

That was why she was on her way to Sittingbourne to spend the weekend with her father. It was time she faced up to things and took control of her life again. It was time she exorcised the ghost of Rashid.

The packed suburbs were giving way to more open countryside. Angela stared hard at a row of trees on the horizon and fought to extinguish the sudden rush of pain that went hurtling through her at the thought of Rashid.

It was because of his memory that she had avoided visiting her father. To see her father was to see Jahira and to remember too vividly all the things she was struggling to forget. And it was because of Rashid's memory that she turned down endless invitations, preferring to spend her evenings alone in her little flat. All she seemed to do in the company of others was make hopeless comparisons and wish she were with Rashid. In the end it seemed less painful just to be by herself.

She breathed in slowly and let her eyes scan the summer landscape. She had been living like this for three whole months now and it was folly to allow herself to wither and die for the love of a man who had never loved her. For, though she could not stop loving him, at least she must start living again. If nothing else, she owed herself that.

This weekend was the first step, she had decided. And the next step would be to go for a drink with Tim next week. She had been putting him off for far too long. And she liked him a lot. It was time she said yes.

The train was emptying with each station they stopped at. Angela stretched her legs, feeling her mood grow more positive. All that was required was that she make a bit of an effort.

She glanced at her watch. In a few minutes they would be in Sittingbourne. And suddenly she was actually looking forward to her weekend. As the train approached the station, she jumped to her feet.

Her father wasn't at the ticket barrier to meet her, but then he had warned her that he might not be. 'I'm due to take the car in for a service and I can't be certain what time it'll be ready.'

'Don't worry,' she had assured him. 'I can easily take a taxi.'

All the same, outside the station, as she headed for the taxi rank, she glanced round quickly just to check if he was there. And her heart gave a sudden bound of pleasure as his shiny blue Rover nudged out of the shadows.

She ran towards it, her bag swinging from her shoulder, and snatched the passenger door open as it stopped alongside her. 'So, you made it after all!' Grinning broadly, she dived inside. But, as the door slammed behind her, her heart stopped in her chest.

Suddenly, she could not breathe. She felt the blood drain from her face.

Rashid smiled. 'Yes, *habibiti*, I made it after all.' Then his brow furrowed a little. 'Aren't you pleased to see me?'

Pleased to see him? She could scarcely believe it! She had expected never to see him again!

But there he sat beside her in an immaculate grey suit, close enough to touch, breaking her heart.

Angela stared at him in a panic of happiness, her expression that of someone who had just seen a ghost. 'What are you doing here? How did you get here?' Stupidly, it was all she could think of to say.

'Your father lent me his car. That's how I got here.' Rashid was smiling at her, strangely, as he said it.

'That's not what I meant. What are you doing in England? And what, above all, are you doing in Sittingbourne?' Surely, she was telling herself, this must be a dream?

'Perhaps I came to see you.' He smiled as he said it, so that she wondered if he had said it as a joke.

'Why would you want to see me?' There was aggression in the question. She must not let him see that she had been dying for the want of him. He must know nothing of what she felt.

'I have a proposition.' He turned away from her. 'We can discuss it when we get back to the house.'

'A proposition?' Angela's heart leapt wildly. 'What kind of proposition?' she wanted to know.

'Be patient, *habibiti*. Now is not the time. I promise I'll tell you when we get back to the house.'

As he spoke he set the car in motion, heading out calmly into the traffic of Sittingbourne, as though he had lived there all his life. Angela frowned at his profile in a tumult of anxiety. Had he really come all this distance just to see her? And what on earth was this proposition of his about?

Her gaze slid to his left hand. He wore no wedding-ring. She felt a flutter of relief and foolish hope go through her. She had neither replied to Mariam's letters, nor even dared to open them, fearing what might be written inside. To have learned that he was married would have killed her.

'I hear you've got a new job.' He flicked her a glance as he said it, a guarded look in the endless black eyes. 'Tell me about it,' he invited.

Angela felt her hope falter on a quiver of suspicion. 'What do you want to know?' she enquired.

'Whether you're enjoying it.' He smiled cryptically. 'I'll bet it's not half as much fun as working for the *News*.'

'It's totally different.' Her suspicion grew sharper, and simultaneously she felt a cold weight in her heart. He had come to offer her her job back. Suddenly she was certain. This proposition of his was purely professional.

Angela turned away abruptly and stared through the windscreen to hide the disappointment that twisted her insides. 'It's a very good job, as a matter of fact.' Somehow she managed to inject into her tone a great deal more enthusiasm than she had ever felt for the job. 'Feature-writer for a big women's magazine. It's very interesting. It gives me a great deal of scope.'

'So, you are enjoying it?'

'Very much so.' Deliberately, she looked him in the eye as she said it. It was, after all, a justifiable lie. Under normal circumstances she would have loved her new job.

'That's good.' He nodded thoughtfully as they turned off the main road. 'I'm glad you found something satisfactory.'

'Entirely satisfactory. I love every minute of it.' He would be disappointed in his mission to lure her back to Jahira, into a situation she had already once rejected. She turned to him stiffly. 'And how about you?'

'Me? I'm just the same.' He slanted her a wry look. 'Of course, they all miss you on the *News*.'

Just for an instant her heart spilled within her. Could it be that he had missed her, too?

But he snatched that hope from her as he added, 'The women's page has managed to tick by, but it doesn't have the flair it had when you were running it.'

There was definitely nothing personal in this visit of his. As she ought to have guessed, it was strictly business.

Without a falter he had reached the gate of her father's little house and was turning in now to the narrow driveway. With trembling fingers Angèla reached for the door-handle, suddenly anxious for the neutralising presence of her father. Being alone like this with Rashid was an unbearable torture.

But, as she hurried through the front door, calling 'Father!' there was no answer.

'He's not here,' Rashid told her, coming up behind her. 'He's gone off for a couple of hours to visit a friend.'

'And why would he do that?' Angela was suddenly hostile. This was his doing! He had set this whole thing up!

'He did it so that we could be private. I told him I wanted to talk to you alone. Don't worry.' He smiled wryly. 'I assure you he volunteered. I didn't throw him out, if that's what you're thinking.'

'Well, there was really no need for him to go off so we could be private, so he could have saved himself the bother!' Suddenly Angela was sick of his manoeuvring. 'You see, I'm not the least bit interested in your proposition!'

The black eyes narrowed for a moment. 'How can you know that when you haven't even heard it?'

'Because I know perfectly well what it's all about. But you're wasting your time. I'm not going back to Jahira!'

They were standing face to face in the narrow hallway that had suddenly become even more claustrophobic than the car. The powerful aura of the tall figure in the grey suit seemed to fill every inch of space between them.

'That is indeed a quick decision.' As he spoke the words softly, just for a moment a shadow of entreaty crossed his eyes. Then he reached out to touch her, making her flesh jump, and instantly Angela leapt back away from him.

'So you're wasting your time if you were hoping to persuade me.' Even to her own ears, her voice sounded shrill. 'There's nothing you can say that would make me change my mind.'

She had thought he might just turn around and leave then. She knew he was capable of such an act. And part of her was hoping that he would, for there was no point in prolonging this useless anguish.

But he did not turn and leave. He looked long into her eyes. Then he turned towards the drawing-room. 'I need a drink,' he said.

Angela followed him mutely with an illogical sense of relief. All this was destined to lead to nothing, for she would not put herself through the torture of going back to Jahira, to work for him and slowly die of love for him, knowing she could never be more to him than a mere employee.

And yet, if he had walked out of that door, it would have taken all her strength not to call him back. This was the last time they would ever have together. It was not a sin, surely, to want to spin it out a little?

She paused in the doorway of the drawing-room as he turned to face her from the centre of the room. 'What would you like to drink?' she managed to ask calmly, somehow overcoming the frantic beating of her heart. The effect he had on her was quite appalling. Three months had passed since she had last set eyes on him, yet she loved him just as fiercely as she had that day in the desert.

'Tonic water, if you have it.' His dark eyes were shuttered as he spoke. Then, as she crossed to the drinks cabinet, he sank down on to the sofa and watched her in silence as she searched among the bottles.

There was plenty of tonic water. She filled two glasses, resisting the urge to spike her own with vodka. He didn't appear to be in need of Dutch courage, so why should she reveal that she was any less composed?

She crossed the carpet silently and held out his glass to him, taking care not to let her fingers brush against his.

As he took it, unsmiling, he held her eyes for a moment. 'So, you're happily settled back into your old life again?'

Angela was glad of the opportunity to turn away from him as she crossed to one of the armchairs opposite the sofa. Her light tone was not entirely reflected in her eyes, as she answered, 'Oh, totally. It's great to be back home again.'

He took a mouthful of his drink. 'So, you were right, after all. This is where you belong. It is good that you have returned to the niche that you love.'

There was a note almost of accusation in his tone. Angela frowned across at him and pointed out, 'Why the surprise? You knew I belonged here. If you remember, you never tired of telling me.'

'Yes, you're right.' He surveyed her for a moment. Then he seemed to force a smile. 'But I am forgetting to tell you the good news about the women's page. Its days in the doldrums could soon be over. I think I've managed to find us a brilliant new editor.'

'A brilliant new editor?' Angela was totally thrown. 'But I thought you were here to——'

'Her husband's recently taken up work in Jahira.' Before Angela could finish, he cut across her. 'She's an experienced journalist, almost as experienced as yourself. MacLeish has offered her the job and she's more or less accepted it.'

'But I thought——' Angela had to lay down her glass. Suddenly her hands were shaking uncontrollably. 'I thought you'd come to offer *me* the job!'

A look of surprise flitted over his face. He shook his head. 'That is not why I came. I would not have come all this way just for that.'

'Then why?' She scarcely dared to ask him. She crossed her hands nervously. 'Why have you come?'

It was Rashid's turn now to lay down his glass. He seemed to sit forward a little in his seat. 'I came to find out how well you'd settled. I thought three months was a reasonable time to wait.' He took a deep breath and narrowed his eyes at her. 'You've told me you're a hundred per cent happy to be back. You have told me also that you would never return to Jahira.' His eyes bored into her. 'That *is* what you said?'

She could scarcely deny it. 'Yes, that's what I said.' And, to her absolute horror, he began to stand up.

'Thank you for the drink. I think it's time I was leaving.'

Without even looking at her, he was heading for the door.

Angela leapt in front of him. 'I was lying!' she croaked. 'I know I said it, but it wasn't true!'

They stood inches apart, the air electric all around them. 'Not true?' he repeated. 'What you said was not true?'

'Not true at all. I'm miserable here. All I do is dream of Jahira and——' She swallowed on the word 'you' and frowned into his face. 'Are you still in love with Lalitha?'

Rashid blinked at her for a moment. 'In love with Lalitha? Whatever gave you that idea?'

'I saw you, remember? In your office.' Angela's heart was thundering. 'What else could I imagine?'

He was shaking his head. 'You crazy woman. Lalitha's my secretary. She's never been anything else.' His eyes were intense as he touched her arm softly. 'What you saw in my office was Lalitha overreacting slightly. I'd done her a favour. She was expressing her thanks.'

'A favour?' Angela blinked at him. 'You mean there was nothing between you?'

'Absolutely not—but I'll explain that later.' He laid his hands on her shoulders, his grip firm yet gentle, holding her there, as he demanded to know, 'Was that the reason you left Jahira—because you believed I was in love with Lalitha?'

'Yes and no.' Angela marshalled all her courage. 'I left because I knew you weren't in love with me.'

He frowned into her face, dark eyes filled with pain, 'You were wrong, *habibiti*. Totally wrong.' He paused to look down at her for a centuries-long instant. 'It is to tell you that I love you that I am here.'

For a moment Angela simply could not speak. Suddenly her whole being was bursting with happiness.

Then she sighed and leaned against him. 'I prayed that was why you'd come.'

'You prayed, *habibiti*?'

'With all my heart.'

She felt the tension in him slacken. He gathered her to him. 'I love you, *habibiti*,' he murmured in her hair. Then, gently, he drew her head back to gaze into her eyes. 'You will be my wife.' It was a statement, not a query. 'There can be no other future for us.'

Angela nodded. No other future. 'I love you,' she told him, drowning in her own happiness. And the words sounded so beautiful she had to repeat them. 'I love you, Rashid. I've always loved you.'

'And I you.' His voice was fierce with emotion. The way he looked at her sent goosebumps down her spine. Then, with a passion that overwhelmed her, he embraced her and kissed her. 'And I you,' he murmured again, thickly. 'For all the days of my life.'

As they came round the corner the lights of the palace seemed to set the night sky on fire.

'Home,' Angela smiled, contentment in her voice. There was no place in the universe where she would rather be.

A hand reached out for hers from the driver's seat of the Cadillac. 'You will never know how much I love to hear you say that,' Rashid told her.

Angela squeezed his fingers, loving the warm touch of him. 'Home is where you are. Home is with you.'

His fingers twined with hers as the Cadillac drew to a halt. He pulled her towards him and kissed her mouth warmly. 'I'm glad we're both home,' he murmured softly. 'I'm glad we finally found each other.'

Angela sighed in agreement and pressed her face against him, breathing in the clean bright smell of him. 'Did you really know, right from the very beginning, that we were destined to be together?' It was a question she had asked him many times before, but she never tired of hearing his answer.

'From the instant I saw you.' He kissed her again, softly. 'I knew that my search was finally over. The woman I'd despaired of ever finding had finally walked into my life.'

Angela tugged his ear playfully. 'No one would ever have guessed it! You tore me to pieces! I thought you couldn't stand me!'

'Ah, but there was a very good reason for that.' He kissed her face softly, a smile in his voice. 'Though *I* knew we were destined for one another, *you* required a bit of convincing. You had come here to Jahira searching for something. I could see that written plainly in your eyes. You thought you had simply come to spend some time with your father. But I knew the truth. You had come to find me.'

He smiled in the moonlight, eyes like black velvet. 'I had to pretend to tear you to pieces. Somehow I had to force you to look into your heart and realise that it was here with me that your future lay.'

Angela nuzzled against him, knowing it was true. It had been written in the stars from the very beginning that her future was with Rashid.

She glanced up and accused him, 'But why did you want me when you kept on telling me that I could never fit in here?'

'I never believed that for a moment. But I knew you were a strong character with firm ideas of your own, and I had to prove—to both of us—that you were capable of seeing other points of view. And I wanted to make you fight for the right to remain here, for it was the only way to make you realise how much you wanted to stay. That was why you had these problems getting your documents.'

'What a sadist you are!' Angela poked him affectionately—for she realised that his judgement of her had been absolutely right. If everything had been too plain sailing, she might easily have taken it all for granted and never realised how deeply her emotions were involved. She poked him again. 'I'll bet you enjoyed seeing me suffer!'

'It was I who suffered!' He rumpled her hair. 'Never knowing for sure what you were thinking about me or if you would ever consider living here in Jahira.'

'But surely by the time I returned to England you must have known how I felt about you?'

'I wasn't sure. I thought you might love me—but I also thought you believed it was something you could overcome. I had to prove to you that you couldn't.'

'So you left me to languish for three whole months! Don't you think that was a little dangerous? I was on the point of going off with that colleague of mine, Tim!'

'So you keep telling me.' He smiled at her, teasing, 'Perhaps you would have been happier if I hadn't come?'

'Oh, don't say that!' Just the thought appalled her. 'You'll never know how miserable I was, believing I'd never see you again. I thought you were lost forever in the arms of Lalitha.'

As she said it she smiled inwardly, feeling a flare of warm pride as she reflected on the true story behind that misunderstanding. How far her suspicions had been from the truth!

Rashid had given her his own modest version, but it was Lalitha's poignantly grateful account that would stick forever in Angela's memory.

'I came to Jahira to forget the man I loved,' Lalitha had recounted to her one day in private. 'I'd always loved him, and he loved me, but he comes from a wealthier family than mine and his parents were demanding an enormous dowry. There was no way my parents could pay such a sum.

'But I couldn't forget him. I was so miserable.' Her lovely eyes clouded at the memory. 'Then Sheikh Rashid generously came to the rescue and offered to pay the dowry for me.' Her eyes lit up. 'I was so happy. I flew straight back to India with the money and my family arranged the marriage.'

'You didn't look happy,' Angela reminded her, smiling kindly. 'You came rushing out of Rashid's office in tears!'

Lalitha blushed a little. 'I was overcome with emotion. No one had ever been so kind or so generous to me before.'

'And you were overcome with emotion again the next time I saw you!' Angela went on to accuse her good-naturedly.

Lalitha's blush deepened. 'I couldn't control myself. I just had to hug him, I was so grateful. Not only had he made my marriage possible, but he'd also gone to the trouble of finding a job for my fiancé over here in Jahira.' She smiled. 'He said it was because he didn't want to lose a good secretary, but it was really because that was what my fiancé and I wanted. Sheikh Rashid really is a very good man.'

'Yes, I know that,' Angela agreed, feeling a warm glow of pride for him.

'I would have told you if he hadn't sworn me to secrecy,' Lalitha assured her apologetically. 'But he said that for my own sake it was better that no one should know.' She smiled then at Angela and confided, 'I think it was also to protect his own modesty. He doesn't like to boast about the good deeds he does to others.'

Her heart swollen with love for him, Angela glanced up at him now. It wasn't just to Lalitha that he had brought happiness. He had given Angela more happiness than she had ever dreamed existed.

She smiled to herself. She had it all: the man she loved, a home that was like a fairy-tale—and, in a few months' time, their first baby would be born, conceived on their wedding-night just twelve weeks ago.

She even had her father installed once more in his villa. 'I'm too young to retire,' he'd quite rightly insisted after revealing his plans to return to Jahira that long-ago evening in far-away Sittingbourne when she and Rashid had announced their engagement.

And, as if all that wasn't already enough, she had a new career, as editorial advisor to the *News*—for it was Rashid's plan to expand the paper's women's interest coverage in the shape of a regular magazine. 'I think the time is right, though we must tread carefully at first. It would only do our cause harm if we were to offend the old guard.'

Angela had kissed him, feeling immensely proud of him. Once she had believed him to be the ultimate chauvinist, but now she knew he was nothing of the sort, rather a fearless pioneer of women's rights. And his way, the subtle way, was the way that worked best.

'Don't worry,' she had assured him. 'I wouldn't harm our cause for anything.'

She stepped out of the car now, and held out her hand to him as he came round to accompany her indoors. He slipped her hand through his arm and smiled down at her. 'You make me very happy, *habibiti*,' he told her.

'And you me,' she answered. 'Very happy indeed.'

'Could I make you even happier?' He paused in the doorway. 'Just speak your wish. All you have to do is ask.'

Angela smiled, her gaze fluttering up to his face. 'I can think of one thing that would give me great pleasure.' Then she reached up to lay a kiss on his chin. 'I would like very much for my husband to make love to me.'

Their eyes held for an instant. A smile passed between them. Then he was sweeping her up into his arms and carrying her across the lantern-lit hallway, up the huge curved staircase and along a wide corridor to a room with a huge silk-covered bed and curtains fluttering by an open window.

As he laid her on the bed, a million stars twinkled. Then he bent to kiss her. 'Your wish is my command.'

HARLEQUIN ROMANCE®

**Harlequin Romance
knows you love
a Western Wedding!**

And you'll love
next month's title in

SHOWDOWN! (#3242)
by Ruth Jean Dale

THE BRIDE was down-home country.
THE GROOM was big-city slick.
THE WEDDING was a match made in Texas!

Available this month in
The Bridal Collection
A WHOLESALE ARRANGEMENT
(#3238)
by Day Leclaire

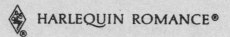

HARLEQUIN ◆ PRESENTS®

A Year
DOWN UNDER

In February, we will take you to Sydney, Australia, with
NO GENTLE SEDUCTION by Helen Bianchin,
Harlequin Presents #1527.

Lexi Harrison and Georg Nicolaos move in the right
circles. Lexi's a model and Georg is a wealthy Sydney
businessman. Life seems perfect . . . so why have they
agreed to a *pretend* engagement?

Share the adventure—and the romance—
of A Year Down Under!

Available this month in
A YEAR DOWN UNDER

HEART OF THE OUTBACK
by Emma Darcy
Harlequin Presents #1519
Wherever Harlequin books are sold.   YDU-J

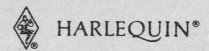

THE TAGGARTS OF TEXAS!

Harlequin's Ruth Jean Dale brings you
THE TAGGARTS OF TEXAS!

Those Taggart men—strong, sexy and hard to resist...

You've met Jesse James Taggart in FIREWORKS!
Harlequin Romance #3205 (July 1992)

And Trey Smith—he's THE RED-BLOODED YANKEE!
Harlequin Temptation #413 (October 1992)

**Now meet Daniel Boone Taggart in SHOWDOWN!
Harlequin Romance #3242 (January 1993)**

And finally the Taggarts who started it all—in LEGEND!
Harlequin Historical #168 (April 1993)

Read all the Taggart romances!
Meet all the Taggart men!

Available wherever Harlequin Books are sold.

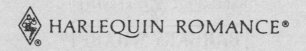

HARLEQUIN ROMANCE®

Norah Bloomfield's father is recovering from his heart attack,
and her sisters are getting married. So Norah's feeling a bit
unneeded these days, a bit left out....

Orchard Valley

And then a cantankerous "cowboy" called Rowdy Cassidy
crashes into her life!

"The Orchard Valley trilogy features three delightful, spirited
sisters and a trio of equally fascinating men. The stories are rich
with the romance, warmth of heart and humor readers expect,
and invariably receive, from Debbie Macomber."

—Linda Lael Miller

Don't miss the Orchard Valley trilogy by Debbie Macomber: